Sisterhood

Maria Arena

Is that how we lived then? But we lived as usual. Everyone does, most of the time. Whatever is going on is as usual. Even this is usual, now.

We lived, as usual, by ignoring. Ignoring isn't the same as ignorance, you have to work at it.

Nothing changes instantaneously: in a gradually heating bathtub you'd be boiled to death before you knew it. There were stories in the newspapers, of course, corpses in ditches or the woods, bludgeoned to death or mutilated, interfered with as they used to say, but they were other women, and the men who did such things were other men. None of them were the men we knew. The newspaper stories were like dreams to us, bad dreams dreamt by others. How awful, we would say, and they were, but they were awful without being believable. They were too melodramatic, they had a dimension that was not the dimension of our lives.

We were the people who were not in the papers. We lived in the blank white spaces at the edges of print. It gave us more freedom.

We lived in the gaps between the stories.

The Handmaid's Tale, Margaret Atwood

"We must continue to unite in sisterhood to turn our tears into triumph, our despair into determination and our fear into fortitude. There is no time to rest until our world achieves wholeness and balance, where all men and women are considered equal and free."

Leymah Roberta Gbowee – Nobel Peace Laureate 2011

Prelude

The Gospel of Sophia 16:7

And God turned his face and lo, the Goddess was revealed.
And she spoke unto them:

All ye who are sisters and daughters of the Goddess, follow my example; unto each other be loving, compassionate, and merciful in the measure of me, God and Goddess; Father and Mother.

On the eastern shore of the black lake, a storm gathered; a towering froth of clouds streaked with blue-white lightning. Thunder rumbled. The air was poised, waiting like the pause between breaths.

In a stone chapel built on the outcrop that half-mooned the western side of the lake, a circle of women murmured a chant as their high priestess prepared for the rite of Renunciation. In their midst, a woman knelt, naked to the waist. Her head was lowered, her face hidden in the length of her hair; her hands rested at her sides. She had been caught by her sisters practicing the macabre arts on a child from the village. The child had lived, as would the woman— although not as one of them.

1

The priestess stepped from the altar and entered the circle, which closed behind her as the women linked hands. A faint silver radiance gathered at each point of connection as the priestess approached the kneeling woman, a white handled dagger held before her. She brought the blade to the woman's breast. The chanting intensified. Beneath the voices of the women, the priestess intoned the prayer of Severance:

Mother Goddess, we return this woman, Caritas, into your wilderness;
Help her find you.
Mother Goddess, we draw the blood of your daughter...

Thunder rent the sky.

Caritas lurched upright, grasping and turning the knife as she rose, and drove it into the priestess' throat. 'Bow before my God,' she said, thrusting the dying woman away. She crashed through the circle, severing the connection between the women.

The storm descended in a fury. The chapel shook, stones falling from the ceiling, breaking the bones of the women who huddled on the floor, calling on their Goddess to take pity. 'Mercy, oh Mother, have mercy.'

Disdain filled Caritas' face as she walked past them. At the door, she caught an object flung at her by the howling wind. A smile twisted her mouth as the stone, lit with the blue-white lightning of the storm, burned into her palm. 'You will not stop me this day,' she said, closing her hand. She hurried to the edge of the outcrop and hurled the stone into the churning lake. As it slipped into the depths, the chapel collapsed.

The storm abated as Caritas strode along a narrow path that wound down the cliff-face. On the shoreline below, two hooded figures waited. When she reached them, one took a robe from a pack and, bowing, handed it over without comment. Caritas shrugged the garment over her shoulders as her eyes travelled the calm surface of the lake. Satisfied, she turned towards her companions. 'Come, sisters, there are girls in the village who require our ministrations,' she said, and lead them into the forest.

Part One

The Book of Faith and Hope

Immanence

Awaken, child, to the dawn,
The glittering 'morrow,
The illusion
Of freedom released.

Capture the restless heart,
The gleaming tower,
wherein resides,
Anticipation's lover.

Seeking the jewelled Spires,
Of a future unbridled,
The dreamer sighs,
Grasps the chimera, laments
The imperceptible day.

The fragile maiden, enticing,
Draws the soul with a promise,
To the glory of her horizon,
Dancing perpetually, out of reach.

On a hill of mist, the fool,
Awaiting the day, yearning,
To embark, to embrace, to live.
In mourning, his despair,
Heavy the burdened,
The dead blossoms of Eventuality.

Chapter One

I want to start by saying my true name is Heather, like the flower, but don't call me that because it'll just bring me trouble. Here, in the Sister's domain, they call me Faith. So – to keep me safe – remember, my name is Faith.

My mother abandoned me at St Mary's Boarding School for Girls one clear autumn morning. In my hand was a bag containing a few favourite outfits, the novel I was reading and an old Bible she'd found somewhere. *It will get you in good with the Sisters*, she said. This wonderful act of motherly love was prompted by a strong desire, on her behalf, to go tramping around Europe with Jeremy Grenouille.

Now there's a name to make a girl shudder.

For the first five minutes, I was actually impressed by St Mary's. The grounds were lush and green with tidy lawns sloping down to the eight-foot high fence enclosing the school. Pines lined the driveway, creating an inviting emerald tunnel that I wandered through, eyes roaming, taking in the details of my new home. Everywhere was trimmed neatness and I wondered how many gardeners it took to keep the grounds in such perfect condition. As I walked, I had the strangest feeling of having stepped out of the real world with its roaring traffic and rushing people, into some sort of fairy kingdom where tranquillity and beauty were always the order of the day. I smiled a little at the thought.

A rustling drew my attention. I scanned the shadowed underskirt of the trees. The darkness deepened as the branches interlaced above me and I felt the weight of watching eyes. I frowned and walked a little faster towards a sun-filled gap in the tunnel, where the pines made room for a church. A large cross sat atop the steeple. Perched on one of its arms was a crow, its head tipped to the side, tracking my movements. As I passed the church, the bird shook out its glossy wings and cawed. I jumped as it was answered by a raucous chorus from the trees behind me.

'Bloody crows,' I muttered.

At the top of the driveway was a small garden with a Poinciana growing in the centre. Leaning against its grey trunk was an old, moss-flecked stone bench. A daydream was born in my mind. I saw myself sitting on that seat, legs tucked up, arms resting on my knees as I read a book in the sunlight filtering through the tree's leafy umbrella.

Maybe this won't be so bad, I thought, ambling towards the convent.

The building the Sisterhood called home was a two-storey weatherboard house, painted a creamy white with a dark blue trim around the eaves. Yellow curtains hung across the windows under which were boxes of aromatic herbs and lavender. Two white cane rocking chairs with blue and yellow cushions sat at a friendly angle on the veranda, a table between them. The convent was picture perfect and had a homely feel as though gentle grandmothers lived there. It was a place where busy, globetrotting parents could leave their daughters with a clear conscience.

Beyond the convent was a three-storey building of dull brown brick. It was set back from the driveway and a little behind the convent, where it seemed to hunch as though waiting to pounce. A short path led to a veranda and a dark unwelcoming front door. This was the dormitory, which was home to the one hundred and twenty girls who were to be my schoolmates. On the far side of the dorm was another brick building, with long grimy windows cut into the side. I didn't look at it for long; it made me feel uncomfortable.

The front door to the convent opened and I turned as a nun dressed in a floor-length black habit stepped onto the veranda. She seemed flustered, as though she'd been busy doing something and had just remembered the time. The nun brushed a hand across her face and adjusted the knotted sash around her waist as she glanced up and saw me.

'Hello,' I called from the driveway, turning on my friendliest smile.

Her brow pinched with annoyance. 'Miss Johnson?'

'Um, yeah, that's me,' I said, my smile slipping.

'You're early.'

I pointed over my shoulder toward the front gate. 'My mum dropped me—'

'Come here.'

My shoulders slumped. *Way to go, Mum*, I thought, crossing the gravel drive. *Get me in trouble before I even unpack my bag.*

Nice.

The nun waited on the top step. *Like an executioner waiting for the condemned*, my imagination insisted. *Shut up*, I told it, looking into the nun's eyes, which were dark and humourless. I searched for a drop of kindness in the pale, angular face framed by the black veil covering her head, but there was no sign of softness. Instead, hers was a face to scare small children and, although I'd

9

turned sixteen three months earlier, I felt my mouth go dry.

As though sensing my discomfort, a smile appeared on the nun's face but, I noticed, it didn't reach her eyes. 'Punctuality is an attribute we cultivate at this school, Miss Johnson. You would do well to remember that arriving before the appointed time is just as rude as arriving late,' she said, tucking her hands into the sleeves of her habit.

I considered telling her that I wasn't the one in a hurry to dump my kid and get to the airport so I could go frolicking with my sleazy boyfriend but, from the expression on her face, I didn't think she'd get it. 'Yes, um, Mother Superior,' I said.

'You will address me as Sister Merce,' the nun said, her voice frosty.

She looked me up and down, taking in my designer jeans and the t-shirt that barely covered my middle (even though I pulled it down as far as it would go), and the sandshoes I'd coloured with green pen one afternoon to pass the time while I waited for my mum to finish one of her endless business meetings. A strand of hair, streaked purple, fell from the loose ponytail I'd tied at the nape of my neck. I slipped it behind my ear and tried not to squirm under that critical gaze.

Just when I thought I couldn't stand the scrutiny for a second longer, Sister Merce clicked her tongue disapprovingly and looked down the driveway. 'I see your mother has left already. Good. You'll settle in more quickly that way.' As she spoke, she came down the stairs, her habit hissing as it dragged over the wood.

I stepped backwards as she stalked past me. I hated doing it but I couldn't help myself. The last thing I wanted was for her to touch me. She marched off towards the dormitory, her back rigid. I hesitated, wondering if I was supposed to follow.

Do you really want to wait for her to ask?

Nuh-ah. I slung my bag over my shoulder and darted down the driveway, keeping what I thought was a respectful distance.

As we walked, Sister Merce delivered her 'Welcome to St Mary's' speech, which went something like:

We are governed by rules here. You will learn these rules and learn them quickly. Failure to abide by them will result in punishment. Three failures in a week and you will be isolated from the other girls until you learn obedience. We do not tolerate insolence in any form. Insolence will be punished by isolation until there is an improvement in attitude. There is no smoking, no alcohol, no drugs and definitely no consorting with males. If you are caught doing any of these things, you will be severely punished and possibly expelled without refund.

As she threw these instructions over her shoulder, the coldness of her voice pressed down on me like a physical thing. I tried to fight against the feeling but, by the time I'd stepped over the threshold to the dormitory, I was on the verge of surrender. I'm not ashamed of that; I've learnt it's the same for all the girls who end up at St Mary's – except maybe the Consecrates, who are a different breed altogether.

Sister Merce charged down the long hallway of the dormitory. I was almost jogging to keep up with her, glancing into rooms as we passed them. One was a dining room, filled with rows of tables. Another looked like a Rec room, while another contained a small chapel. At the end of the hallway were rooms with closed doors. I sensed something foreboding lurking down there and I was relieved when Sister Merce turned up a flight of stairs about two-thirds of the way down the hall.

Young girls – juniors, I guessed – moved to the side of the staircase and seemed to cling to the banisters as the nun clumped up the stairs. They kept their eyes averted. On the second floor was the junior dormitory. A nun stood on guard in the doorway; the girls inside sat in pairs or alone, reading, writing, drawing, knitting (*yeah, I know*). The low, rhythmic murmur of voices followed me up the stairs to the third floor, where Sister Merce turned into a long room, full of silent girls standing at attention by the end of their beds.

The seniors, I thought, as the nun walked between the two rows of girls, her 'welcome' speech droning on even though I had stopped at the door. My gaze jumped from solemn face to solemn face. Something was missing from the room and it took a few seconds to work out what it was: Hope.

Chapter Two

Once upon a time, in an era long, long ago, Prince Charles attended Timbertop, that swanky private school in Victoria. When my mother, who has an unhealthy obsession with royalty and fairy tales, discovered this bit of trivia – thank you, Google – she decided her kid was going to a school that had a similar philosophy.

Lucky me.

When I was in grade eight, she started showing me web 'brochures' from all-girl schools and colleges around the city that she felt fitted her ideals. I didn't pay much attention; before my mother met the Frenchman (and his millions), she was always blabbering on about some new 'path' we could take to better our lives. But I was happy at my school, and I didn't want to change to some snobby, elitist prison, especially one without boys, so I ignored her – proving that when you stick your head in the sand, you end up with a kick in the butt.

Or you end up in a place like St Mary's which, believe me, ain't *nothing* like the brochures.

St Mary's girls were expected to work hard and achieve high. To help maintain the school's stellar academic standing, classes began at eight in the morning and finished at five in the afternoon, with a one-hour study period after dinner, followed by a compulsory half hour of free reading before lights out. 'Free reading' sounded good in the advertising material, but it was a misnomer since the Sisters decided what could be read, and you can bet *Harry Potter* didn't make their list.

Classes took place six days a week, although on Saturdays students could finish at midday, providing they had some type of 'appropriate' sporting or cultural activity to attend. On Sunday, the students went to Mass at seven, followed by an hour of spiritual reflection. Sunday afternoons were devoted to maintaining (read: *cleaning*) the dorm and other areas of the school. No minute was spare at St Mary's; idleness wasn't in the Sister's vocabulary.

Neither was the term 'social media', which was reinforced by a strict technology policy. When my mum read about it on their webpage – which is darkly ironic, when you think about it – she could hardly contain her enthusiasm.

'Look at this, Heather. Oh, this is brilliant. It's exactly what you need.'

I pulled my gaze away from my laptop screen; my best friend, Samantha, had just sent me a message on Facebook, detailing her date with Johnny Bishop. I'd caught the phrase *like a groper* as I looked up, and it took all of my willpower not to ignore my mother and keep reading.

'What do I need?' I asked, the message tugging at my mind. *Sam, what wickedness have you been up to now?* I wondered, feeling a delicious thrill for my friend.

'St Mary's has a no technology policy,' my mother said. I stared at her, watching the words forming on her lips, but my face was blank; she could have been speaking Martian for all the sense she was making. She saw the expression and turned her laptop towards me.

I read the page, my forehead squeezing into a disbelieving frown. 'They can't do that.'

'Apparently they can,' my mother said, almost gloating as she leaned over her laptop and tapped a section of the webpage. 'See, here: No television. No internet. No email. No mobile phones. No digital cameras. No iPods or iPads. No video games. No laptops.'

'That's stupid. How am I supposed to study?'

She read for a moment. 'Not a problem. St Mary's have their own laptops and Intranet that has filters to block out "Facebook and other unacceptable Internet sites."'

'No way. What is it? A gulag? How am I supposed to talk to my friends. There's no way I'm going there,' I said, as another message from Samantha arrived. I pulled my laptop closer and hunched down behind the screen, hoping my mother would stop talking and leave me alone.

I got half my wish as she stood and walked towards the kitchen. As she reached the doorway, she stopped and looked at me. 'You'll go where I tell you, my girl,' she said, and my stomach clenched when I saw that stubborn smile she wore when she was determined to get her own way.

That's it, I thought, *I'll be enrolled at St Mary's before the week's out.*

But, no.

The best thing about my mother is her attention span; she's like a goldfish, one loop around the bowl and she's forgotten where she started. Still, I kept quiet on the subject of schools, sensing I'd escaped a fate worse than death, but then Mum met *Le frogman* and, although I didn't know it, my days as a free girl were numbered.

As bad as I thought St Mary's would be from its website, in reality, it was a thousand times worse. The school was like the Titanic; it looked like a good idea but turned out to be an inescapable disaster, with no hope of rescue. The minute the gates shut behind a new arrival, they were cut off from the outside world. As the website promised, there was no Internet and no TV, but there was also no newspapers or magazines. When something 'newsworthy' happened – a terrorist attack, a change of government, the overthrowing of a dictator (forget Hollywood and all that 'sinful guff') – the girls heard about it from the Sisters in the daily announcements. Or from the new arrival, if they could get to her before the Sisterhood.

This was the second thing I learnt on my first day at St Mary's: information has a currency.

I got through dinner that night, although I couldn't say what I ate. I could feel the eyes of every girl watching me. Not outright, not staring – only the Sisters were open about their inspection, which was creepy because of its intensity; I felt like a lamb being drooled over by a bunch of wolves (which is not too far from the truth). Instead, the girls watched me from under blunt fringes and lowered eyes. They stole glances as they picked up glasses of water, or forked food into their mouths. Theirs was a silent, sneaky assessment that was just as hungry as the Sister's obvious scrutiny.

Both made me want to bolt for the exit, but what would be the point? My mother was winging across the Pacific with Mr Sleazoid, and there was no knight in shining armour on the other side of the fence. I was stuck, with no option but to wait for whatever came next.

I realised later that something was watching over me that first night, as the Sisters were occupied with their other pursuits. This doesn't happen often, maybe once a month. Usually the Sisters prowl the dormitories, ready to pounce on anyone who isn't following the rules, and there are a lot of rules at St Mary's.

Having the Sisters out of the dorm provided the girls in the beds beside me with an opportunity. The bidding started about ten minutes after lights out. I didn't know what was going on at first; the dormitory was filled with urgent whispers, of which I caught fragments:

'…biology test on Friday…'

'…cleaning for a week…'

'…three chocolates for one…'

'…take the blame…'

In the dimness of the room, I saw the girls either side of me shake their heads, rejecting offers, or pausing to think over an option. The whispering continued with a fierce urgency:

'…decide now…'

'…hurry, or we'll be…'

'…caught…'

The girl to the left of me rose up on her elbow, pointed across the room, and lay down again, but it was the girl to my right who asked the first question, preceded by a warning. 'Stay still, answer directly and don't speak above a whisper.' She stared at me in the gloom, waiting for me to answer. I nodded and she continued, 'Have you read *The Book Thief*?' I nod again. 'Does Liesel fall for Rudy?'

I looked around the dormitory. *This is what they want to know?* I wondered, taking in the eager faces watching me, hanging on for my answer. 'Umm I don't know. I didn't finish the book,' I said.

There was a low disappointed groan from somewhere further down the row of beds, which was interrupted by the girl on my left, who fired off a question about some grunge rock band I'd never heard of. I shrugged, 'Sorry—' The girl glared at me and turned away.

The questioning went on for another ten minutes, and I answered as best I could, until a commanding whisper came out of the dark. 'Enough.'

A silence as final as a full stop filled the dorm. I looked at the girls to the left and right of me, but their eyes were closed, their chests rising and falling in what I assumed – wrongly – was an imitation of deep sleep. In the months to come, I would learn their trick, which would save my sanity on more than one occasion.

If I thought the questioning session would make fitting in easier, I was wrong. The next morning, the girls ignored me as they went about their routine in silence, their every move watched over by the Sister standing in the doorway. She didn't speak either but there was a tension in her body as her black eyes touched each girl, and I knew in my bones that she was waiting, hoping, for one of them to slip up. The same tension held the girls rigid; their movements were almost robotic, but fast and efficient.

I followed their example, dressing, washing and making my bed as quickly as possible to avoid finding myself in the glare of the Sister's attention. When the room was pristine – my mother would have called such neatness a miracle – the girls lined up and followed the sister to the dining room for breakfast.

Falling in behind them, I moved in close to the last two girls. 'Hey,' I said, keeping my voice low and watching the sister at the head of the line. 'Is there anywhere I can go for a run?' I asked.

'Don't talk to us,' muttered the dark-haired girl in front of me.

The pretty blonde girl next to her glanced at me and looked away. I caught the hint of a smile and felt better. 'What are you called now?' she asked over her shoulder.

'Huh?'

She exchanged a look with the girl beside her. 'What name did the Sisters give you?' she asked, emphasising each word as though she was speaking to a moron. Her friend giggled.

'Oh,' I replied, remembering Sister Merce's final comment from the night before: *From now on, as a sign of your new life here at St Mary's, you will be known as Faith and you will answer to no other name except Faith.* Before I could respond, the nun had swept out of the dormitory, leaving me wondering if she was serious. From the look on the blonde's face, I guessed it wasn't a joke.

'Faith,' I said.

'Well, Faith, we don't run at St Mary's.'

'Oh,' I said, feeling the twist in my stomach that I get when I can't train. 'Is there a track nearby?'

The dark haired girl made a low impatient sound and the blonde touched her wrist to silence her.

'No one leaves the grounds.'

'But—'

'It's for your safety,'

'But—'

'Shut up,' the blonde said, her voice low and sharp as a slap.

So much for making friends.

I've never had heaps of friends; no one would crown me Miss Popular, that's for sure, but I'd always had a couple of close girl-buds, like Samantha from my last school, and Chloe and Brigitte from my old neighbourhood, to hang with and share the gossip. Maybe that's why the first month at St Mary's was so damn hard. I was a freaking pariah and I didn't understand why. I guess that's what drove me to approach Sister Anna-Marie, who seemed younger and nicer than the other Sisters, to ask if I could call my mother.

What was I thinking?

Don't ask me.

While I knew my mother probably wouldn't even answer the phone, I needed to hear a familiar voice, even if it was thousands of kilometres away and coming from the bottom of a martini glass. She didn't get the chance to disappoint me.

Even as the question left my lips, I saw Sister Anna-Marie's eyes widen as she looked over my shoulder. I didn't need ESP to know who was breathing down my neck.

'You are dismissed, Sister.'

Sister Anna-Marie nodded and hurried away without looking at me again. I turned, readying my reason for wanting to speak with my mother, as I faced Sister Merce.

Black eyes. No smile. No compassion. No chance.

'Telephone calls from students to the outside world are prohibited.'

'But I really need to talk to my mum,' I said, trying to control the whine in my voice.

'Do you? Poor pet.' The nun's gaze bored into my face. 'I can appreciate your need,' she said as her tongue darted across her lip, 'but we have one hundred and twenty girls in this school. Can you imagine the cost if we let all of them ring their parents the moment they were feeling a little blue?'

She had a point, damn it.

'Can't you make an exception?' I asked, tasting the saltiness of tears at the back of my throat. *Don't you cry in front of her*, I told myself.

'No.'

What a bitch.

'Look, I just—'

The sister moved closer to me and drew a slow

21

breath. For an instant, I felt like she was pulling something out of me, some invisible essence. I tried to fight the idea but every nerve in my body shouted: *stay still, stay quiet* as though I was a field mouse and she was a hovering hawk. Then her eyes narrowed and she said, 'I don't care.'

Sister Merce stepped away and I could move again. I leaned against the wall, feeling weak and quivery in my legs as I did after a twelve kilometre run. The nun smoothed down the front of her habit and her manner became blunt and businesslike again.

'We have a telephone policy at this school. Parents may contact their daughters one Saturday evening per month between 7:15 and 8:15 with prior arrangement, or without notice, in the case of an emergency. This was outlined in the school's welcome package.'

I pushed against the wall, trying to stand straighter. 'I don't think my mother read that section,' I said.

'I guess you're on your own then,' Sister Merce said, not bothering to hide her smirk.

Oh mother, what have you gotten me into here?

The old nun was right; I was on my own but I wasn't the only one. All of the girls at St Mary's – even the Consecrates, who didn't have friends so much as followers – were isolated and alone. I watched them; sure they interacted, worked together, ate together and all that kind of stuff, but none of them were friends in the way we could be friends in the outside world. There was no chat about boys, or fashion, or make-up. There were no beauty sessions, painting nails and doing hair, and there were no D&M's with junk food overdoses to make us feel better. The Sisters watched us too closely for any of that as they filled up our days and nights with their never-ending 'educational and personal development' tasks. We were busy, and busy girls had no time to make connections.

After the loneliest month of my life, my hope of finding a friend had faded to the sickly yellow of an old bruise. By the night of the Bethany incident, I thought it had disappeared forever.

We'd been asleep for an hour when our dormitory was flooded with harsh white light. I snapped awake, as did the girls around me. No one slept through an 'incursion' by the Sisters if they wanted to avoid being the target of their special ministrations. I saw straight away that I didn't have to worry about my own skin because, standing in the aisle between the beds, surrounded by three Sisters, was the youngest inmate at St Mary's.

Bethany was one of those pixie girls; everything about her was delicate. Her arms and legs were slender; her face was small and framed by short dark hair. The only thing large about her was her eyes, which were stretched open with terror. She was in her nightgown, and it was obvious that she'd been ripped out of her bed and dragged here without explanation. Her head turned from sister to sister, a plea on her face as she shivered.

Sister Merce spoke from the shadowed doorway and every girl in the room leapt from their beds and stood at attention. 'One of you is responsible for writing graffiti on a pew in the chapel. Confess or you will be responsible for what happens to this child.'

A gasp flittered around the dorm joining Bethany's low cry as two of the Sisters grabbed her arms, while the third – Sister Patrice – brought a thin bamboo rod from behind her back. As I searched the faces of the girls, and they searched mine, looking for the culprit, I wondered if any of them were stupid enough to do such a thing. I didn't think so. Who'd want to make their life harder than it already was?

'You have one minute to confess,' Sister Merce

23

said, coming down the aisle towards Bethany. I caught the malice in her eyes and suddenly, I knew; there was no graffiti.

A sick feeling plunged into my stomach as I looked around the room at the other girls and saw that they knew the lie too. Sister Patrice passed the rod to Sister Merce, who smiled into Bethany's tear-stained face.

I couldn't let it happen.

But, before I could step out of line, another girl – Agnes – spoke up. 'It was me, Sister.'

The dorm fell silent, as though all of the girls had taken a collective breath. A flash of annoyance flicked across the nun's face as she rested her cold gaze on Agnes. She made a wet, clicking noise with her mouth and dropped her hand on Bethany's shoulder. 'We have our graffitist,' she said, as the girl released a sob. 'Back to bed for you, little one.'

Bethany fled. Sister Merce curled a finger at Agnes. 'Come, girl.'

Agnes didn't look at us but her chin was raised and, although I saw her mouth tremble, she didn't cry.

I prayed that night, though I'd never done so before. I prayed for Agnes. I prayed for escape. I prayed for strength, for hope, for salvation. I prayed to my mother, but mostly I prayed to a God who I sensed had no place at St Mary's.

Call me foolish, but I had to get help from somewhere.

Chapter Three

Like an answered prayer, Hope arrived on a warm Saturday afternoon.

I was in the attic above the dormitory; a dusty room over the sleeping quarters, forbidden to us girls by the Sisters. They'd boarded up the entry long before I was dumped at the school, but a few planks and some rusty nails were never going to stop me getting where I wanted to go. My mother, with her amazing "astrological wisdom", would've put this down to my being a stubborn Taurus. In reality, the attic was the only place at St Mary's where I felt I could breathe. It was a sanctuary and, although I knew there'd be hell to pay if I was caught, some things were worth risking.

From my vantage point, I watched Hope – as the Sisters later named her – approach the convent. Her hair was loose and shifted across her shoulders as she scoped the grounds, curiosity obvious in the tilt of her chin. I moved closer to the single round window and looked across to the convent's veranda; the hem of Sister Merce's heavy black skirt was visible beneath the eaves.

This'll be interesting.

Girls who ended up at St Mary's could be divided into three groups. At the top were the Princesses (the spoilt product of super-rich parents). Second in rank were the Abandoned (girls dumped here by high flying, globe-trotting, corporate parents too busy to worry about something as trivial as a daughter). My mother, as part of said jet-setting class, sent me postcards from little towns across Europe. The last one had a picture of a lake nestled between two snow-topped mountains somewhere in Geneva. These cards were usually filled with empty sentiments that she expected me to hoard like precious gems. Sometimes they were blank. Either way, I looked them over once and tore them to pieces.

At the bottom of the hierarchy were the Wayward. They were girls who'd slipped through the cracks: recovering addicts, runaways, foster brats, street kids, who the Sisters took in as part of their "pastoral duty". None of them last long at St Mary's.

Mostly, I could pick the category a new girl would fit into by the way they behaved when they arrived at the school, but the girl on the driveway was different. To begin with, she'd arrived without parents.

Intriguing.

Princesses were typically brats when they first arrived, turning their backs on their well-meaning parents and stomping into the dormitory like they owned the place. That attitude lasted until they met Mary and her consecrates. Goodbye snootiness; hello compliancy.

The Abandoned were the opposite of the Princesses; usually they had to be coaxed or dragged away from their parents. They knew what it meant to be handed over to the Sisterhood – well, at one level anyway. The minute Mummy or Daddy's car door closed, *bam*— welcome to postcard central.

I'd never seen a Wayward arrive at St Mary's; we'd wake up in the morning and there they'd be in the dormitory. Later, they'd vanish without causing a ripple in our routine.

Hope arrived alone, like some fearless goddess.

I felt a flutter of excitement. *At last*, I thought, *someone with potential.* Below me, a door creaked and Sister Anna-Marie hurried down the dormitory stairs. She took a few quick steps along the path before she glanced at the convent and saw Sister Merce. Indecision caught her mid-stride, making her sway, before she pirouetted and scurried back into the dormitory.

Oh yeah, just another wacky moment at St Mary's.

I guess I shouldn't be too hard on Sister Am (as we call her – although never in front of the other nuns) since she's the nicest of the Sisters. She's about twenty-five, although it's hard to tell since the cornette she wears pulls her skin tight across her face, smoothing out any tell-tale wrinkles. She's sweet and always has a kind word, not like the rest of the Sisters, whose faces would crack if they even attempted a smile.

I pressed against the window as Sister Merce came down the steps and launched into her speech. Hearing the words wasn't necessary; originality wasn't one of the Sisters' strong points. Still barking out the rules, the nun brushed past her new charge and started towards the dormitory. Hope shrugged as she turned to follow.

Here is where the surrender begins.

But instead of shrinking under Sister Merce's rant, Hope seemed to *grow* with each demand. Her back straightened and her head came up, like an aristocrat on her way to the guillotine— which was how she came to see me.

Hope stopped in the middle of the driveway and looked up at the window, apparently forgetting about Sister Merce, who continued to stalk towards the dormitory confident her charge was behind her. I pulled back, putting shadow between us, hoping she would think her eyes were playing tricks on her and move on. After a moment, I looked down at the driveway again.

Hope was still staring up.

Damn.

I glanced towards Sister Merce.

The nun had also stopped when she realised Hope was no longer following her: no longer *listening* to the rules, no longer *obeying*, and she was *turning* to see what had happened to the new arrival. I looked at Hope and frantically pointed towards the Sister, praying she would understand. For one long second, she continued to stare and I thought my heart would explode with panic, until she dropped to one knee and began fiddling with a silver anklet. She unclasped it and popped up again as Sister Merce completed her turn. The nun spoke and Hope sent a glance in my direction as she handed the anklet over.

Clever girl.

A frown of annoyance creased Sister Merce's face; God may have given the students of St Mary's free will, but Sister Merce was the one who decided when we would use it.

If Hope saw the thunderous look on the nun's face she pretended not to notice as she sauntered over to the steps leading into the dormitory. I lost sight of her beneath the eaves but from the sound of the screen door banging and the look on Sister Merce's face — which would have been belly-hugging funny on *anyone* else — I could tell she'd gone inside. I watched Sister Merce, fascinated to see what she would do, yet terrified for Hope.

The Sister stood still, hands clenched at her sides. She drew a breath and held it. Her fingers flexed, tightened, flexed. The tension subsided. She breathed out and shook her head before marching to the dormitory.

I dropped away from the window and lay on the floor. The blouse under my tunic was stuck to my skin and I pulled it free with a grimace. That was too close, I thought as the first murmurings of girls returning to the dormitory came through the floorboards beneath my head. They would've been ordered there by Sister Merce.

Crap.

How could I forget the Parade?

I scrambled over to the narrow stairwell that lead down to the dormitory, dodging the squeaky last step as I slipped between the boards covering the entry to the attic. On the other side was a supply cupboard where the "feminine products" and linens were kept. The cloying scent of deodorised cotton made me gag. I breathed in shallow sips until I crept from the cupboard and closed the door.

A Wayward – I think her name was Joy – gave me a dull look as I entered the room. It had been a week since her last hit of speed and the ghost of her addiction haunted her face. Over her shoulder, I saw more girls arriving and I quickly moved to the end of my bed. I smiled at Joy, but her expression remained vacant.

What a waste.

I sighed as I focused on the hairline crack in the window on the opposite side of the room. The other girls had also taken up positions at the end of their beds and they stood at attention, waiting for Sister Merce. I still hadn't figured out what the Sisters hoped to achieve with this display of military-like conformity. I guess it was supposed to reinforce the self-discipline expected at St Mary's. If that was the case, it wasn't working on me. My eyes kept drifting to the door where I knew Hope would soon appear, but first came Sister Merce.

Butterflies with razor wings took flight in my belly. The nun moved down the aisle between the beds, making sure we were complying with her rules. Her cold gaze flicked past Joy, crawled over my face, before shifting across to the bed opposite where it connected with Mary Henna.

Mary was a Princess and Sister Merce's favourite Consecrate. Their eyes locked and an unspoken message past between them.

In another life, Mary had been christened Michelle, but she wore the name given to her by the Sisterhood like a beauty queen's sash. As I watched the strange interaction, I thought about the Sister's obsession with our names. I guessed it was something like the Nazis did to the Jews, stealing their names away and turning them into numbers, making them less human and easier to kill. Name changing was all about control.

At first, I'd thought of resisting but, after watching Sister Assumpta force a girl to eat a block of Sunlight soap for using her real name, I decided it wasn't worth the trouble. Hell, it wasn't like I'd be called Faith forever, was it? No, just until I finished Grade Twelve, or my mother decided to bail me out of this joint.

Great.

Just as my usual cloud of melancholy descended, Hope swept into the dormitory. With her came the subtle sounds of agitation: an intake of breath, the scrape of a shoe, the rustle of a skirt.

The heavy tap of Sister Merce's booted foot against the floor restored silence.

I leaned forward, peeking around Joy, daring to watch Hope whose eyes flashed with curiosity as she scanned the rows of girls. I felt a thrill at her boldness but when I realised she was searching for me, I ducked back and returned my gaze to the window, hoping for anonymity.

Too late.

Hope strutted towards Sister Merce, who was standing beside the only vacant bed in the dorm. As she passed me, I heard a murmur; an indecipherable acknowledgement that meant: *I recognise you.* I bit the inside of my mouth to keep from smiling.

'Girls, you may sit,' Sister Merce said. There was a clumping of feet as we took a step to the side and one backward, which brought us to the edge of our beds. Then, as one, we sat.

All eyes turned to Sister Merce. 'Today we have the pleasure of welcoming a new initiate to our family. Girls, this is Hope. She will be with us for a while, so make her welcome, teach her the rules and ensure she is included on the work roster. Mary, you will be responsible for disposing of these garments' – the word came out with a sneer – 'and replacing them with a uniform. For tonight, Hope will attend to table duties. Faith, you will show her what to do and ensure she makes no mistakes.'

Neither Mary nor I responded to Sister Merce's demands; our acceptance was a given. She nodded, satisfied, then turned to Hope and muttered something that, although I strained to hear, was audible only to her. I watched Hope's face and, as Sister Merce turned away, I saw that her pale skin had taken on a ghostly sheen. She sat on her bed and stared at the nun's retreating back.

Welcome to paradise, I thought as I stood and went over to her. It was time for dinner and the nuns were very particular about the way their table was set. 'We have to go down to the dining room now. There's a lot to do before the 5.50 warning bell.' I shifted from foot to foot like an impatient child. When I realised what I was doing, colour flushed into my cheeks.

Not that Hope noticed; a crease of concentration had appeared between her brows. I reached out and waved my fingers in front of her eyes. She blinked and looked at me, a tentative smile appearing out of her frown. I didn't like that hesitation and I wondered if my intuition was wrong. Had her indifference as she walked up the driveway to her encounter with Sister Merce been an act to cover the fear she was really feeling?

There was no time to discover the truth. The nuns would be on their way to the dining room shortly and if my chores weren't done, there'd be hell to pay. 'Come on,' I said, nodding in the direction of the door, 'we've got to get downstairs.'

'Okay, keep your shit together,' Hope said, as she stood.

A chorus of gasps echoed around the room. I stared at Hope, my throat sandpapered with fear. At the same time, my heart soared. *Not an act*, I thought and smiled.

'What?' Hope asked.

Before I could answer, Mary shoved past me and wrapped her hand around Hope's arm. 'Your table chores will have to wait, Faith,' she said. 'I'm taking Hope to get a new uniform.'

'Hey, get out of it,' Hope said, pulling free.

I stepped away as Patience and Gertrude came to stand beside Mary. Gertrude glanced at me, her heavy shoulders twitching apologetically as she shuffled closer to Hope, boxing her in. Patience stood on the opposite side, her eyes fixed on Mary.

Alone, the twins were pleasant enough and some-times we'd hang out together – especially when Mary wasn't around. They were from a small country town west of Longreach and the bush was written into their bodies. When I listened to their slow, melodic laughter, I pictured them riding sturdy horses, chewing on shafts of wheat, Akubra hats protecting them from the sun as they rounded up stray cattle on their parents' farm. The reality was probably a lot different – private tutors, church socials, cocktail parties – but I liked thinking of them that way; as simple, wholesome girls.

Things changed when Mary was around, and she and the twins were doing the Consecrate thing. Then I stayed away, since being on the receiving end of one of Mary's cruel punishments wasn't my idea of fun. As, it seemed, Hope was about to find out.

'Get the fuck away from me,' she said, as Patience and Gertrude pressed against her. The demand was met with another chorus of gasps. 'I'm not going anywhere with you.'

'Really?' Mary asked, her voice soft.

Hope turned to face the Consecrate, her expression calm. Mary returned her stare with an equal measure of serenity. The atmosphere was stifling; no one stood up to the Consecrates. Ever.

The Consecrates lived amongst us, shared our dormitories and bathrooms, ate at our tables, went to class and sat through Mass. They blended in but were different too. I'd been trying to figure out what made them so special. It wasn't that they were rich (although they did come from wealthy families) or that they were particularly attractive (except for Mary), or intelligent, or even all that wicked (difficult to judge since, according to Sister Merce, we were all 'bad' girls in one way or another) yet they lived among us with the air of the Chosen. Whenever they walked past, conversation stopped. If one of them wanted something, no matter how precious to its owner, she got it. When a Consecrate told us to do something, no matter how unfair or degrading, we did it without complaint.

Why?

The answer was simple: the Consecrates were the eyes and ears of the Sisterhood. They monitored our every move and reported back to the Sisters. In return, they were spared the harsher treatment that was doled out to the Abandoned and were protected in a way that the Wayward could only pray for. This privileged position made them dangerous and Hope – without understanding what she was doing – was provoking them.

The tension between the girls was a blister and I knew I had to do something before it burst. Hope had no idea what she was getting into; the Consecrates could be merciless. I closed my eyes for a second, gathering my determination, then stepped between the girls.

'Don't worry about it, Hope. Get the uniform and I'll meet you in the dining room later. You can learn the routine tomorrow.'

Mary's steel grey eyes remaining locked on Hope as she said, 'How wise of you, Faith.'

I didn't answer. Enflaming the situation was pointless.

Hope, on the other hand, was more than happy to push the issue. She thrust out her hip, the denim of her jeans straining over the jutting bone as her shirt pulled up, revealing the ring she wore through her belly button. 'The uniform can wait. I want to help you with whatever you're supposed to be doing.'

For a moment, no one spoke. We stared at Hope: at the tightness of her jeans over her hip, at the flash of bare stomach, smooth and creamy, but mostly at the sparkle of jewellery dangling from the centre of her belly. She reminded me of what was beyond the walls of St Mary's; of what it was like to be a girl in the real world.

A frown rose on Hope's face. 'What the fuck is with you people? Quit staring at me, you're creeping me out.'

Gertrude moved first. She buried her fist in Hope's stomach as though she was groping for the belly ring. 'We don't use that sort of language here,' she said, as Hope grunted and doubled over.

Another sigh floated around the room, this one filled with release, as though Gertrude's violence had somehow restored balance to our lives. The other girls scrambled for the door with a renewed sense of urgency. 'Don't you have something you should be doing, Faith?' Mary asked.

I looked at her and bit my lip. God, how I hated everything about her: the flintiness of her eyes; the way her blonde ponytail curled over her shoulder like an inverted question mark; the perfect curve of her fingernails; the smug turn of her mouth; the way she could make anything look glamorous, even the limp uniforms we were expected to wear. If St Mary's had its own fashion magazine – called *IMMACULATA* maybe – Mary would be the cover girl. More than anything, though, I hated it when she was right. I had to get downstairs, but I didn't want to leave Hope. She was still doubled over and I could hear the rasp as she dragged air past her solar plexus.

'Don't worry, we'll take care of her,' Mary said. If that was supposed to reassure me, it wasn't working. Mary knew it – and didn't care. She stared at me, waiting.

A loud ticking, like an amplified metronome, drew my attention to the clock above the dormitory door. I glanced at it, noting the second hand as it marked off the moments to disaster. There was no more time to waste. 'Just remember she's new and doesn't know how things work around this place,' I said, spitting the words at her, wishing they had the power to wound.

Mary lifted a perfect eyebrow in reply.

Chapter Four

I skidded into the dining room seconds before Sister Am appeared. She looked at the empty tables and then at me, her expression questioning.

'I know Sister. I'm very sorry. I was helping the new girl settle in and didn't see the time. I'll have it done in a jiffy.' I started towards the cupboard beneath the windows where the dinner settings were kept but, at that moment, Hope and the Consecrates walked past the dining hall door. She glanced at me; her skin was luminescent, but there was fire in her eyes. A smile twitched at the corner of her mouth and then she winked at me before disappearing down the hallway.

'Faith? Did you hear me?'

I turned to Sister Am, a frown pulling at my brow as I tried to think of what she may have asked. 'I'm sorry Sister. What was the question?'

'Are you paying attention now?'

'Yes Sister.'

'Good. In that case, I said, "What is the new girl's name?"

As she spoke, I opened the cupboard, took out a tablecloth, and began to roll it down the length of the first table. 'Her name is Hope.'

'Lovely,' Sister Am said, smoothing a corner of the tablecloth while I went back to the cupboard for the second one.

When the other table was covered, I took out the first stack of plain white plates. They made a soft clatter as I placed them on the table. I glanced over my shoulder at Sister Am but she only nodded for me to continue as she followed along the row, positioning each plate to perfection.

Next was the cutlery. I opened the drawer and scooped out a handful of knives that glinted in the fluorescent light. One of the Sister's favourite punishments was for disobedient girls to polish the cutlery until it shone. A simple task most thought, until they realised there were over a hundred and forty sets of knives, forks and spoons, and that was before they started on the teaspoons. I'd seen girls who entered the dining room swaggering reduced to tears as their hands began to throb after an hour of polishing. By the end of the second hour, with another three drawers to go, most would be promising to follow the rules of the Sisterhood to the letter.

As I put the last knife into place, I took a quick look at the clock and felt my heart skip. Only twenty minutes before dinner and there was still so much to do. I silently cursed Mary and rushed over to the drawer again, this time taking a handful of forks, holding them to my chest like a posy. My legs shook as the metronomic ticking started again, mocking me. Panic made me clumsy and the forks clattered against the plates as I set them on the table. I looked at Sister Am again, expecting her anger.

But the nun was walking the length of the second table, placing a fork beside each perfectly positioned plate. She saw me staring and tilted her head. I remained still for a few moments; the Sisters never helped us with anything and I knew Sister Am was risking the wrath of the other nuns if they caught her. That was enough to get me moving. I flew down my table, setting each place as fast as I could.

My thoughts turned to Hope as I worked. In my time at St Mary's, I hadn't met a girl like her. The way she stood up to Mary and the Consecrates took guts. Then there was the way she'd been with Sister Merce. That was weird. What had the old nun whispered in her ear? I wondered. I'd never seen Sister Merce speak to any new girl like that. She mostly gave her speech and palmed the newbie off to the Consecrates, as though the girl was beneath her consideration. Had she recognised some special quality in Hope?

I'd seen so many things during my time at St Mary's – some I didn't understand and others I didn't *want* to understand – and I'd been searching for someone to share these secrets, but none of the girls seemed suitable. Either they were Consecrates (or one of their stooges) or they were so terrified of the Sisters that even the hint of confrontation sent them over the edge, or running to the Sisters.

So I kept what I'd seen to myself. The problem was, the pressure of everything I'd witnessed was building inside me until some days I felt like screaming. To relieve the strain, I watched and waited in my secret room, hoping each new girl who passed through St Mary's gates would be the one I could connect with before the Sisterhood tainted her.

Was Hope that girl?

Time would tell.

I placed the last fork and went back to the cupboard for the glasses. Like the cutlery, these sparkled as though they'd magically appeared out of a 1950s dish-washing commercial and I almost expected to hear a crisp 'cha-ching' as I placed them on the table.

'Make sure those glasses are centred, Faith.'

'Yes Sister. Sorry Sister,' I replied, wondering what Hope would have said. *Fuck off, Sister*, most likely.

A wave of guilt washed through me. Sister Am didn't deserve my uncharitable thoughts. Still, I couldn't help feeling a touch of elation; finally there was a girl I could talk to about the horrors at St Mary's.

Sister Am stayed until I finished, then excused herself. I thanked her repeatedly for helping me and probably would've hugged her too, except that would be crossing a line I wasn't sure I wanted to step over. The nun smiled and told me to hurry.

As befitting their elevated opinion of themselves, the Sisters sat at a table on a raised platform overlooking the students. This table was set with a white lace cloth, pale blue china, sparkling silver cutlery and delicate teacups decorated with tiny pink and blue roses. Each setting had to be exact: knives and forks a centimetre from the edge of the plate, cup four centimetres from the top of the plate with the handle turned to the window. The precision was crazy but, as Sister Merce often explained, 'Discipline is in the detail'.

Of course, my mother would've said, "The Devil is in the detail," but who was I to argue with a nun?

From the platform, the Sisters watched as we ate our meal of boiled potatoes, cabbage and carrots, and a piece of meat of unknown origin. It was nursing home food – nourishing, but as bland as cardboard. None of us looked forward to mealtimes, no matter how hungry we were. Still there was no point complaining since the Sisters ate the same food, spooning it into their mouths like automaton.

Charming.

I turned the last cup handle towards the window and looked over the tables. Everything seemed to be in place.

'So what's so bloody special about setting tables?'

Self-preservation is an amazing instinct. When I heard Hope's voice, I spun around, my finger touching my lips to shush her, as I leapt from the platform, crossing the distance between us as though I'd suddenly developed superpowers.

'Didn't you learn anything from Mary?' I whispered, coming up close to her. 'You can't go around saying whatever you like here. In fact, we shouldn't even be speaking at all. If they catch us, we'll be punished. And don't think being new will get you off, because it won't. No one is exempt. No one.'

'Okay, chill out. I get it,' she whispered and was quiet for half a breath. 'But if we aren't allowed to talk, how the fuck are you supposed to show me what to do?'

I rolled my eyes. 'Jesus, you *are* asking for trouble.'

'Oh, I see how it is. It's okay for you to blaspheme but I can't swear?'

'No, it's not okay but, well, you— you can't go around saying— Oh forget it. Take a look around, note everything, because this is how the nuns expect the tables to be set, morning and night.'

She moved away, wandering the length of the room, her eyes roving. I knew she wouldn't remember everything but I hoped she'd get enough of an idea to keep her out of trouble. The weekly roster would be posted after dinner and, since I'd been on dining room duty for a week, Hope would be working with someone else tomorrow. Unless the nuns decided to set her some other, more difficult task, which was likely since the Consecrates would've reported her behaviour in the dormitory.

'Okay, looks pretty straight forward,' Hope said, as she came back to where I was standing. 'Now what?'

I raised an eyebrow, liking her confidence but

wondering how long it would last. 'Now we wait for the Sisters and everyone else. Then, you'll have the pleasure of tasting St Mary's cuisine for the first but, unfortunately, not the last time.'

Hope smiled. 'Is the food that bad?'

'Worse.'

She groaned and then fell silent as the door behind the Sisters' table opened and Sister Assumpta swayed in. The nun was almost as wide as she was short and her habit clung to her like the skin of a sausage, bulging in the oddest of places.

'What are you two doing in here?' she demanded as she heaved her body onto the nearest chair. It creaked in protest and I heard a stifled chuckle beside me.

'We're on dining room duty, Sister,' I explained, praying she hadn't heard Hope.

Sister Assumpta glared at us, her eyes raisins in the doughy folds of her face. I held my breath. It wasn't wise to underestimate any of the nuns, but Sister Assumpta could be particularly dangerous, especially if she thought you were making fun of her generous girth. She shifted in the chair again, deliberately making the legs squeal as she watched for our reaction.

I kept my eyes focused on a spot in front of the platform and redoubled my prayers as I listened for Hope's snort of derision. It didn't come. Instead, the door opened again and the other nuns swept into the room. Sister Assumpta gave us one last contemptuous glance before turning to Sister Merce, who took the chair beside her.

I took Hope by the elbow and pushed her over to the table closest to the window as the girls entered the dining room in their straight, silent rows. When everyone – students and nuns – was standing behind a seat, Sister Merce recited the evening's blessing. Her voice was stern, as though she was delivering a final judgment rather than a prayer of gratitude. She ended with an 'Amen' that had the force of a blow. We sat, as one, and waited without talking for dinner to be served.

That meal was the most difficult I'd experienced at St Mary's. The tension built inside me, making the food even harder to swallow. I pushed the colourless peas to the side of my plate, their wrinkled skins causing my stomach to flip in revolt. Leaving food was forbidden, but I just couldn't force them down. I kept expecting Hope to say something like, 'Did we really give thanks for this crap?', but she kept her head down and forked food into her mouth as though she hadn't eaten in a week.

At first, I was relieved until I began to worry about why she was eating so fast; was she trying to attract attention? I watched her from the periphery of my vision. She was up to something and I wasn't the only one who sensed it. On the other side of Hope sat Philomena, a dark haired girl with the disposition of a mouse. She kept glancing at Hope and shuffling along the bench seat, widening the gap between them. Her face was creased with concern and I wondered why. Then I understood.

Oh God.

The sound had been easy to miss amid the other noises in the dining room. Subdued as we were, one hundred and twenty girls eating at once created its own cacophony, but as the other girls finished their meals and silently placed their cutlery on the table, the harsh clunk of Hope's fork against her plate rang out like a bell in a steeple. I glanced over at the nuns, who were still preoccupied with their meals, although Sister Am – who was sitting closest to us – was frowning at the distraction. As I watched, she looked in our direction.

Philomena was pushed up against the girl next to

her. Bernadetta also shuffled away from Hope. A vision of the girls tumbling off the bench filled my head and my stomach clenched with fear.

Around the room, girls – alert to danger – shifted in their seats as the Sisters turned towards us, carnivores sniffing fresh meat. Hope's fork continued its rhythmic beat against the bottom of her plate. I bit my lip, wondering what to do. Any sudden movement would be spotted by the Sisters, making me the target of their ministrations – something I was happy to avoid – but I didn't want Hope getting in trouble either. I gathered my courage and tapped Hope on the shin with my foot.

'Shit!' she yelped, reaching for her leg although I barely touched her.

The room broke into chaos.

Bernadetta tumbled off the end of the bench, taking Philomena with her when she grabbed her arm to keep from falling. They let out twin grunts as they landed in a tangle beside the Sister's platform; the other girls were on their feet, some giggling nervously, others moaning as they peered at the Sisters.

The Sisters!

Silence descended; a silence so complete it was as though we'd been plunged a thousand metres underwater.

Every eye fixed on the nuns. The moments stretched. Finally, Sister Merce spoke, 'Resume your seats. Faith. Hope. Philomena. Bernadetta. Join me in my office at the conclusion of dinner.'

The room filled with sound again as the girls slid onto the benches. Philomena and Bernadetta scuttled up from the floor, their eyes filled with tears as they lowered their heads in submission. I looked at Hope through half-closed eyes, warning her not to make the situation worse. She raised her eyebrows, unconcerned.

On the platform, the nuns resumed their seats as Sister Merce said, 'Let us pray.'

I didn't hear the prayer. I was too busy worrying. I knew Philomena and Bernadetta would get off lightly – probably bathroom duty for a month – but I had a bad feeling about what Sister Merce would serve up for Hope and me. I knew what happened to girls who broke the rules. I'd heard the stories about them going missing only to reappear days later, bruised and compliant – if they came back at all. I shivered as Sister Merce finished the prayer.

'You may go with God's grace girls, and no more mischief.' She left the threat hanging and walked from the room.

The other girls stood and slipped away to prepare for Rec hour, leaving Philomena, Bernadetta, Hope and me in the dining room. We huddled together in the doorway, looking down the hallway to Sister Merce's office. A large silver cross hung to one side of her door. On the other side was a painting of the *Sacred Heart*. I tried to take comfort in the kindly face and open arms of Jesus, but his bleeding heart only reminded me of what waited for us in Sister Merce's office.

'Well? Are we going?' I glared at Hope. 'What?' she asked, all innocence, 'it was just a question.'

'Whatever,' I snapped and took the lead.

We approached the door slowly and I felt my body leaning backward as though straining against some invisible barrier. My heart was doing a crazy jackhammer dance and I could feel Philomena and Bernadetta breathing against my neck. I wanted to tell them to back off, but the sound of voices coming from Sister Merce's office drew my attention.

The door opened and Sister Am stepped past us. She glanced at me and I frowned. *Has she been advocating for us?* I wondered, as she strode away, leaving us to our fate.

Philomena and Bernadetta were called in first.

'What's going to happen to them?' Hope whispered, as the door closed.

'Don't talk to me,' I replied, staring after Sister Am.

'C'mon, don't be like that. Maybe there's more going on here than you realise.' She smiled in the gloom.

'Have you lost your mind?' I muttered and held up my hand. 'No, I don't want to know, just stand there and be quiet. We're in enough trouble. We don't need to be caught talking as well.'

Hope was about to respond anyway, but Philomena and Bernadetta rushed out of Sister Merce's office, silencing her. Their faces were ashen. They fled down the hallway and hurried up the stairs to the dormitory. I watched them go and looked at Hope, wondering if she finally understood how much trouble we were in. From the playful glint in her eyes, I could see she still had no idea. I groaned under my breath as Sister Merce called our names.

Chapter Five

The Sisters lived by two principles: repentance through hard work and discipline through frugality. These principles were supposed to lead to a state of purity and connection with God. Nice in theory, but in practice, it sucked.

Their principles meant uniforms made of cheap synthetic material, complimented by heavy, all-purpose black shoes that redefined ugly. "Vanity is the province of the Devil," Sister Merce was fond of saying. If that were true, I'd happily move suburbs.

We slept on beds made from pine with thin mattresses that drooped between the slats. We showered in water with a hint of heat, which was a blessing in summer but torture in winter, and had our three plain meals a day.

Complaining about the conditions we lived under was pointless because the Sisters shared our way of life. To them, there was no better way to show their dedication to God. Personally, I thought three Our Father's, a Hail Mary and a gold coin donation would've worked just as well – but what do I know?

Sister Merce's office was a shrine to austerity. A sturdy wooden desk sat on the far side of the room; a high-backed chair in imitation leather was pushed back against the wall, as though recently vacated. On one corner of the desk, an old lamp with a forty-watt bulb threw out a weak yellow light, creating more shadows than illumination. Hope and I clumped across the timber floor. The nun stepped out of the gloom by the window and took her seat, folding her hands over a spotless ink blotter as we came to stand before her.

There were two other objects on the desk: a Bible and a pair of black handled scissors with silver blades. The Bible was open and covered in a delicate script that I couldn't read. When Sister Merce saw where my eyes had ventured, she closed the book, making a heavy *thunk* as its pages came together. She pushed it aside and refolded her hands in front of her. The gesture was patient; as if she had all the time in the world to deal with us.

Her demeanour made me jittery, like a woman on death row or a bride about to make her vows ('Different day, same outcome,' my mother would've said) and I glanced away, wishing she would get on with it. On the wall behind her, a painting of the Virgin Mary – the *Mater Admirabilis* – hung in an elegant frame.

Subtle as a brick in the face.

I studied the painting showing the Virgin Mary enthroned. Her hands were folded in her lap and her eyes were downcast in contemplation. A halo of stars surrounded her veiled head. Beside her was a lily in a vase, a spinning distaff and, by her feet, an open book resting on her sewing basket. She was the picture of passivity and self-control, and as I gazed on her peaceful face, I felt a rush of guilt.

So not me, I thought.

Sister Merce tapped her fingers against the blotter and I looked at the carpet, the painting working its magic. Hope shuffled but I stood to attention and she took my cue, growing still beside me.

'You've had an eventful first day,' the nun said, addressing Hope, who shifted but kept quiet. *Was she finally learning?*

'Not as eventful as some days, Sister. Isn't that why I'm in here?'

Nope.

To my surprise, I heard a chuckle. I raised my head, thinking someone had entered the room – maybe Father Joachim from the deep timbre of the laugh – but there was just the three of us. I glanced at Sister Merce and felt a shock of disbelief. She was smiling at Hope; a sinister expression for sure, much like the one a shark wears before it bites its victim in half, but still, a smile.

Oh Hope, what are you doing?

The nun stood and picked up the scissors as she came around the desk. 'There are many reasons why young women end up at St Mary's, my dear, but I can assure you, by the time you leave—' The smile flickered again. 'You will have repented and embraced the light of the Lord.' She raised the scissors as she caught a thick strand of Hope's hair. I held my breath.

This was the Sister's favourite punishment: cutting the hair of girls who broke the rules, shaming them with ugliness – although it was usually reserved for more serious offences like consorting with males or going AWOL. I looked at Hope expecting to see fear, but she just watched Sister Merce as though daring the nun to do her worst.

A moment before the scissors began their work, Hope said, 'I already walk in the light, Sister. *Ad maiorem Dei glorium, Adsum.*' She lifted her hair from between the blades and locked eyes with Sister Merce.

I risked a glance at Hope. *Was that Latin?*

The tension built and goose bumps rose on my arms. Not even the Consecrates dared to stand up to Sister Merce and even her own Sisters deferred to her judgment. Yet, here was a girl who'd only been at St

Mary's for a few hours and she was engaged in a battle of wills with the nun, which she appeared to be winning.

Suddenly, the window on the far side of the room rattled with the beating of wings as a crow flung itself furiously against the pane. My stomach leapt and I saw Hope jump at the sound. Sister Merce snapped her head towards the window.

'Satis,' she hissed. The bird gave a raucous cry before flapping away.

The nun turned back to us, her face composed. 'We'll see the strength of your light soon enough, child,' she said, clicking the scissors in front of Hope's face before dropping them on the desk. 'Do you remember what I said to you upstairs?' she continued, not waiting for a reply. 'You should think about that and moderate your behaviour during your stay with us. After all, there are many ways to encourage you to follow the path of righteousness.'

Hope smiled. 'Whatever you say, Sister. Is that all for tonight?'

My mouth dropped open; was there no end to her boldness? I waited for Sister Merce to explode into a fury but again she refused to be baited. 'I'm afraid not, Hope. There is the small matter of your disruptive behaviour at dinner,' she said, turning her gaze on me. 'And don't think I've forgotten about you, Faith.'

Without thinking, I let my chin sink and fixed my eyes on the floor, bringing a low murmur from Hope but I wasn't concerned. I knew there was something special about the girl next to me, but she didn't know the Sisters like I did. I'd been burnt before and I was determined not to let that happen again. Yet, even as this thought passed through my mind, I realised that somehow Hope *did* know what Sister Merce could do and that she either didn't care, or was deliberately trying to provoke her.

Why she wanted to do that, and how she even knew about the Sisterhood, was a mystery that pricked my curiosity and made me feel defiant. I lifted my head and stared at the cross hanging around the nun's neck.

Sister Merce narrowed her eyes and, in a voice that indicated her annoyance with my newfound confidence, explained our punishment. 'There is no excuse for what went on during dinner this evening. Although you are new to our school, Hope, the other girls set a fine example for you to follow but you chose to ignore it. And you, Faith, have been here long enough to know how to stay out of trouble. Dinner is a time for peaceful contemplation of the bounty provided by God, a chance to express our gratitude. By your actions, you have shown a profound disrespect for God. In order to repent this sin, you will report to Sister Assumpta in the gymnasium after morning prayers.'

I closed my eyes and sighed, knowing what was in store for us; repentance through hard work.

Great.

With Sister Assumpta, whose favourite past time was making girls clean until their hands and knees were bleeding and raw.

Fantastic.

In the gymnasium that hadn't been cleaned in, let's see— forever.

Brilliant.

Cleaning the gymnasium was just how I wanted to spend my Sunday; like it wasn't bad enough having to slave all week in class learning French and stupid algebra or the whole bloody history of ancient Egypt. I glanced at Hope to see if she was pleased with her efforts and found her smiling again.

What was with her?

It seemed Sister Merce was asking herself the same

question and feeling as exasperated as I was, for she turned in a flurry of black material and picked up the scissors again. She grabbed a length of Hope's hair, wrapped it tightly between her fingers, and jerked. Hope cried out but didn't resist and, in an instant, Sister Merce had hacked off the strand.

Hope regarded the nun. I waited for her reaction, though I was long past knowing what it would be; the whole interview with Sister Merce was like nothing I'd experienced before.

After my first few encounters with the Sisters, I learnt it was easier, and less damaging to my health, to keep my head low and at least appear to be following the rules. It was not in my nature to be submissive but to survive the Sisterhood and their special ministrations, I knew I had to be creative in my subversion of the nuns' authority.

Hope, on the other hand, was blunt in her defiance and I wondered whether her behaviour was a deliberate ploy to draw the Sisters out? But, if that was her intention, why was she provoking them? Who was she? What was she doing here? And why had she singled me out? The questions raced through my mind but only Hope could provide the answers.

I shifted impatiently as Hope and Sister Merce stared at each other. Finally, Hope broke the standoff. She shook her head, then took a band from around her wrist and quickly pulled her hair into a ponytail, the jagged edges of the missing strands sticking out; a statement of her defiance that was not lost on Sister Merce.

'Report to Sister Assumpta in the morning and mind you do exactly as she says,' the nun said, her voice taut. 'Now get out of my office.'

I grabbed Hope by the arm and pulled her towards the door before she had a chance to say anything more.

She came willingly enough, but I noticed that she couldn't resist shooting one last look over her shoulder as we passed into the hallway. I don't know what Sister Merce's reaction was but the slamming of her office door told me she was unimpressed.

As we reached the stairs, Hope slipped her arm from my hand and smiled as she clunked up the steps. 'Hope, please,' I whispered, taking church-mouse steps, 'we've been in enough trouble tonight.' She glanced at me and shrugged as she brought her foot down softly on the next stair. I offered a small prayer of gratitude when we reached the dormitory without one of the Sisters breathing fire and brimstone in our direction.

Sister Constance, who was on dorm duty for the month, lifted her eyes from the patchwork quilt she was working on, her gaze passing over me and coming to rest on Hope. Her mouth twitched as though trying to remember how to smile before falling into its usual placidity. She returned her attention to her stitching and began humming as her fingers walked over the fabric on her knee.

It was agreed amongst the girls that Sister Constance, while harmless when compared to the other Sisters, was as loopy as an amusement park ride. I wasn't so sure though; did disappearing inside yourself to escape the ugliness infecting the world make you crazy? It seemed like a reasonable strategy to me. There were times when I wished I could burrow deep inside myself and only come out to make the world a little more beautiful, which was what Sister Constance did.

The only time she looked truly alive was when she played the organ at Mass, her fingers finding a purity in the notes that was so sweet, my head hurt to hear them. Her eyes would sparkle and delight would light up her face. She was almost beautiful – until Mass ended. Then she slipped away again, aware of her Sisters and her duties towards us girls, but not really with any of us.

The dormitory was a hive of near-silent activity. Girls sat on their beds in their identical ankle length nightdresses, keeping busy with our approved tasks — reading, writing letters to parents, or sewing and knitting. Some of the girls were finishing off crocheted blankets and macramé baskets that would be sold at the school fete later in the year, their fingers moving slowly as they tied the intricate knots.

As Hope and I entered the room, all eyes turned to us. Unspoken questions filled the air. I knew they were wondering how we'd survived our encounter with Sister Merce. Before stepping behind the "modesty screen" beside my bed – *gotta love those Sisters* – to strip out of my uniform, I looked over at Hope and asked myself the same question.

Chapter Six

Routine is a comforting thing. It lets you know the tempo of your life; how each moment will be used as you're drawn towards the end of the day. When the lights were turned off at nine o'clock – as always – I closed my eyes and sighed. From the first bed in the dormitory, Sister Constance hummed the Lord's Prayer for about fifteen minutes, when the sound of her voice was replaced by the gentle rhythm of her snoring. I turned on my side and gave in to the fuzzy warmth creeping over my body.

I didn't hear Hope approach until she placed her hand on my shoulder. Her touch yanked me from the edge of sleep. She put her hand across my mouth, smothering my yelp before it had a chance to live. I looked at her in the gloom as she put a finger to her lips.

As if she had to tell me to be quiet.

'We need to talk,' she whispered.

I nodded and climbed out of my bed, pointing to the door at the end of the dormitory. Hope frowned but followed as I crept past the rows of sleeping girls. I moved slowly, listening for any change in their breathing, knowing Orwell's *Big Brother* was alive and active at St Mary's. The Consecrates were the worst for it; not that they had exclusive rights on spying and informing

– all of us were encouraged to report on any girl who broke the rules. I moved with exaggerated care until we reached the supply cupboard.

As I turned the knob, the latch made a soft snick and I froze, waiting to see if anyone heard. The silence held. Hope nudged me and nodded as if to tell me to get on with it. Rolling my eyes at her, I pulled the door open and stepped into the darkness. I felt my way to the back of the closet, using touch to find the release for the panel.

'Cool,' Hope whispered, following me into the attic.

The half-moon provided enough light for us to cross the support beams, arms out for balance, and reach the window at the far end, where we sank down on the floor. Hope surveyed the attic but I looked outside, over the pine trees to the real world beyond the wall. Glittering lights danced like fairies in the distance, glowing aureoles of red, green, orange and blue, interspersed with vivid purple, candy pink and flashy orange.

I felt a tug in my heart, remembering shopping trips into the city with my mother when I was younger that always included a late afternoon movie at the Dendy. The film was usually something foreign, with subtitles that I didn't read because I was too captivated by the women parading across the screen: African, Indian and Asian beauties with smouldering eyes that seemed to hold a secret knowledge.

When the film was over, Mum and I would stroll downtown amid the carnival of lights and have dinner at the Delphina Club and then onto Buson's for hot chocolate. I never wanted those nights to end. Even though my mother spent much of her time on her mobile or chatting to friends, she would often send a glance my way and smile at me through her cigarette smoke, and I would know that she saw me.

I sighed and thought of my mother now, sipping champagne on some yacht as she sailed around the Caribbean. She was a scrawled name on a postcard. I pushed her out of my mind and turned to Hope.

Her eyes roamed over my face. I wanted to squirm under her inspection, but I controlled the urge and waited for her to finish. 'What's your real name, Faith?' she asked.

A blank space opened in my mind. It seemed a lifetime since I'd even thought of myself as anyone but 'Faith', a lifetime since anyone had called me anything but 'Faith', and I realised how efficient the Sisters had been in all but eradicating my identity.

Damn it. I thought I was being so rebellious, so strong, so resilient but they had been cunningly undermining me all along. I gazed at the lights over the city again, picturing the streets, the theatre, the movie stars, until it came to me. 'Heather,' I said, smiling. 'My real name is Heather,'

'That's pretty. Were you born in the Bay?' Hope asked.

'The Bay?'

'Byron Bay. You know, alternative capital of Australia, where they're into Mary Jane.' I gave her a blank look. 'Umm, Marijuana?'

'Oh right. No, I was born in Brisbane. I think my mother named me after Heather Locklear. Priscilla was a big fan of *Melrose Place*.'

Hope frowned. 'Who's Priscilla and where's Melrose Place?'

'Priscilla is my mum and *Melrose* was only the biggest show on TV in the nineties.'

'I stopped watching TV when I was eight.' It was my turn to frown – *no TV?* – and Hope shrugged. 'One of my teachers told me it's all lies and propaganda presented as lifestyle choices, so I watched for a bit longer and saw he was right. It's a bunch of one dimensional images pretending to be real people, telling us how to live our lives. Who needs that crap filling your head?'

'Oh okay, well, there you go.' I floundered. 'So, it looks like you and the Sisters have something in common after all; a shared hatred of television,' and I mentally slapped myself even as Hope shook her head, making her hair tumble around her face.

'I have nothing in common with them. And, by the way, my name is Amy and when we're not around the Sisters, I want you to use it, okay Heather?' She fixed her eyes on mine.

That squirming feeling was back. Here was a girl who could be my ally in the struggle to survive the Sisterhood and I didn't want to disappoint her, but I couldn't agree to her demand. 'You don't know what they're like,' I said, my voice tight as though the words had fingers that were pressed against my throat. 'If we slip up in front of them—'

Hope held out her hand, silencing me. 'I have some idea what the Sisters are like,' she said.

I thought she was referring to the interview with Sister Merce and I shook my head, ready to disagree. She had *no* idea.

'And that's why we have to rebel in any way we can.' She paused, her eyes losing focus as though she was listening. A faint nod brought her back to the attic. 'But maybe there are other ways to fight the Sisterhood, so okay – Faith, it is.' She turned to the window and seemed to be listening again.

Did she say fight them? A chill touched my skin but I didn't know if it was fear or excitement. When she looked back, I said, 'Sorry about the TV thing.'

'Forget it. There's more important stuff to talk

about.' Hope stretched her legs out in front of her and then pulled them under her nightdress. She crossed her arms over her knees. 'Tell me what you know about the Sisterhood.'

Now there was a million dollar challenge: where to start? I'd learnt much during my captivity and overheard much more; stories from the other girls and rumours that drifted down the corridors like spider's silk. Some of them I believed, but others were so horrible they couldn't possibly be true.

Are you sure? a voice whispered in my mind.

I shivered, ignoring the question, and started my story in the time before I came to St Mary's. 'My mother fell in love with a Frenchman. His name is Jeremy and I loathed him on sight. He was always going on about the places he'd travelled to, and the famous people he'd met, and how great his kids were— back in France. It didn't occur to him that everyone's kids were wonderful when they were on the opposite side of the world. Then he told me how well they were doing at their *boarding school.*

'I guess that should've tipped me off but, although she'd mentioned it before, I never thought my mother would seriously consider the idea of sending me away. So much for family loyalty, huh? Anyway, a month later, here I am.'

'How long have you been here?' Hope asked.
'Seven months longer than forever.' I leaned my head against the wall, needing to feel something solid. 'The first week was the worst, as it usually is for everyone. Except the Consecrates.'

'Yeah, what's with them? How come they get special treatment?'

I shifted, the floorboards growing uncomfortable. *How much should I share with her?* I wondered. *How much would she believe?* I decided on the truth.

'They're the Sister's chosen ones, handpicked because there's a darker side to them that you don't want to cross. Like with Mary. She's gorgeous on the outside and she can be nice in that smarmy used car salesman's way, but get on her bad side, or if the Sisters tell her to target you, she's vicious.'

'I can handle her,' Hope said.

'I noticed, but it's early days; it'll get worse. And she's nothing compared to the Sisters. Those women are cold-blooded, especially Sister Merce. You need to be careful of how you deal with them.'

Hope put her hand across mine. 'What did they do to you, Faith?' she asked.

My throat locked up, but Hope was waiting, her eyes curious. I took a breath and forced the words out. 'I'd been at St Mary's for three months. Things had settled into a routine and nothing really bad had happened for a while, though there was always this sense of something impending, you know, like a trap waiting to be sprung.'

'Like in a *Tom and Jerry* cartoon?'

'Yeah, something like that,' I said, and laughed a little. 'Anyway, Sister Constance was on bed duty this night, which was the reason I was able to get out of the dormitory in the first place. I woke about one in the morning and I could hear crying. At first, I thought it was one of the girls in the dormitory, but it grew louder.

'I sat up and looked at the other girls, but none of them even twitched. *You're hearing things*, I thought until the pain-filled cry came again. I was out of bed and sneaking past Sister Constance before I considered where I was going. By then, it was too late to stop. I started down the stairs, wondering if it was one of the juniors, but their dorm was as silent as a tomb. At the bottom of the stairs, the cry came again and I followed it along the hallway, passed Sister Merce's office, to a door tucked into a shadowy alcove. Then came a drawn-out whine and I froze.

'Every inch of me was yelling "Get the hell out of here" and – I know it sounds bad – but I wanted too. After all, whatever was going on behind the door was none of my business. And it wasn't like I was friends with any of the girls, so why was I playing the hero? I stepped back but the cry came again; louder this time, as though whoever was behind the door knew I was there. How could I turn away?

'I wrapped my hand around the doorknob and, in that instant, the door was wrenched open and I found myself staring into Sister Assumpta's eyes. Shadows leapt across her face, distorting it into an inhuman mask. I took three or four quick steps backwards until I crashed up against the wall.

'You mightn't believe me, Hope, but she *pounced* across the hallway. I shrunk away, sure she would smother me with her bulk, but instead she gripped my arm and demanded to know what I was doing out of bed.

'I couldn't reply, and when I felt her nails sink into the soft flesh behind my elbow, I thought I would faint. She dragged me towards the stairs, half carrying me when my feet tangled in my nightdress. We stumbled into the dormitory, waking the girls who sat up and watched. Sister Assumpta flung me onto my bed before turning to Sister Constance, who was still sleeping peacefully. The fat nun shook her Sister awake— '

'Stop. Wait,' Hope said. 'Who was in the room?'

'I never found out.'

'But the crying?'

My shoulders twitched. 'You get used to it.' Shock settled over Hope's face and I felt my defences rising.

'Things happen to some of the girls here that no one questions,' I said. 'That's just the way it is.'

'Well, *someone* must question. Parents? Friends?'

'The Wayward don't have parents and friends, that's how they end up here. No one cares about them on the outside.'

'The Wayward?' Hope asked.

'The girls who cry in the night, the ones who disappear. The ones the Sisters—' I shook my head. 'You don't understand, but you will,' I said and rushed on before she could dig deeper. 'Sister Merce hunted me down the next morning, catching me outside the kitchen.'

'"What were you doing out of bed last night?" she asked. I told her about the crying. "That was your imagination," she said and when I said I didn't think that it was, she squeezed my wrist until I gasped.

'"Don't think, Faith. It'll get you into trouble and troublemakers don't last long here." I looked into her eyes and knew I had to escape, no matter what.

'"I want my mother," I told her, feeling like a five year old on their first day of school. It was humiliating and pointless. Sister Merce didn't even bother to respond and, as she walked away, I promised myself I'd find a way out.'

I paused, surprised at how easy it was to recall that night. At the same time, I wondered if Hope believed me about the crying. It sounded bizarre and I was afraid she would laugh at my wild imagination, but when she spoke, there was no hint of disbelief, only acceptance, which was somehow more frightening.

'You couldn't get away though, could you?'

'Not through lack of trying.'

'How many times?'

'Just once,' I said, and felt blood rush into my

cheeks. Now she'd laugh or, worse, leave. Instead, she stayed where she was, waiting for me to go on with my story. 'I waited a week after that night. I'd kept a low profile, quietly going about the tasks the Sisters set and staying out of trouble. At the same time, I searched for a way out; trying to come up with an escape plan and maybe even find someone to help me, but most of the girls here are already dead.'

'What do you mean?'

I hesitated, wanting to get the point right. It felt important, as though it was some sort of test by which Hope would judge if I was the one she was looking for. 'Well, I don't mean they're physically dead. I'm not talking *Zombieland* or anything like that.'

'Good movie,' Hope said.

'Yeah, cool zombies.'

'Shame about the geeky leading men.'

'True, but stella zombie-killing chicks.'

'Yep, they kicked zombie arse, for sure,' Hope said with a smile. 'So, we're not talking about the living dead wandering the halls of St Mary's?'

'No,' I said, returning her smile for a moment before it faded away as I searched for the words to explain the girls who were in the care of the Sisterhood. 'It's more like they've realised that whatever is here is bigger than anything they can handle; that it's too powerful for them to overcome so they've given up. They're dead on the inside, do you see?'

Hope nodded. 'But there still might be some redemption for them, and for us.'

Redemption?

'Who are you?' I asked, the question slipping out before I could catch it.

She waved it away. 'That's not important right now. Tell me about the great escape.'

I wanted to disagree; who she was and why she was

at St Mary's seemed like the most important thing in the world. Still, I put the question aside and continued. 'Six days after I began the search, I found a way out. I'd just finished cleaning the windows at the back of the convent – Sister Assumpta's idea; she's such a peach – and I was climbing down the ladder when I noticed a section of the wall surrounding the school grounds leaning outwards. I put my bucket down and, after making sure no-one was watching, I wandered over to check it out.'

'What was it?'

'A gate. Very old and held in place by the ivy. I pushed and there was a protesting squeal as it shifted a few inches. Through the gap, I saw a road. That was it; my escape route.

'I thought about waiting for a few days before bailing, but the word around the dormitory was Sister Dolorosa was taking over night duty. That was enough to convince me to go that night.

'Everything went fine at first, except I almost threw up every time there was a noise I didn't recognise. Still, I was feeling pretty confident by the time I reached the convent. Only a dozen steps to freedom; I could almost feel the bitumen beneath my feet. I was squeezing through the gate when they caught me.'

'Damn,' Hope said, and drew a breath. 'What happened?'

I hesitated before answering. This was the hard bit; the test. Would she think I was crazy? Or would she believe me? I bit my lip and plunge on with my story.

'Sister Merce wasn't human when she dragged me back through the ivy.'

'You mean, she was inhumane?' Hope asked, leaning forward.

I fidgeted under the intensity of her gaze. 'I mean

she wasn't human. Her face was sort of twisted, de-formed, and there was something about her eyes. They reminded me of a cat, the pupils were elongated, yellow, maybe. I'm not sure. There was something else but— I passed out.'

'You fainted?'

'I didn't mean to,' I snapped.

'No, no, I'm sure you didn't,' Hope said, squeezing my arm. 'I'm sorry, keep going.'

I shrugged, not looking at her.

'Really, I'm sorry.'

'Okay,' I said.

Hope relaxed her hold on my arm but her fingers remained against my skin, comforting and encouraging. 'Do you remember anything else?

'Just the look in her eyes.' I shivered. 'Hatred; pure, black, cold hatred.'

A thoughtful expression crossed Hope's face and she drew away from me. 'And what was she like when you woke up?'

'Normal, or as normal as Sister Merce gets.' I shook my head and focused on that night. 'She brought me around with a slap, and then Sister Assumpta dragged me up to the dorm, where the girls and other nuns were waiting.

'It was like some bizarre sleep-over party. The girls were standing in a circle in the middle of the room. In the centre of the circle was a chair and Sister Con-stance, looking terrified. Sister Merce shoved me onto the chair and, while two of the Consecrates held my arms, she took her black scissors from the folds of her habit.'

'The ones from tonight?' Hope asked.

I nodded. 'Sister Constance shook her head when she saw the scissors. Sister Merce ignored her and turned her attention to the girls. She rattled off some bullshit about expectations and lessons but I hardly heard her. I was busy watching those scissors. I didn't know, you see, what she was going to do with them and my mind was full of slasher-movie violence.'

Hope reached out and brushed the jagged ends of my fringe. Sadness touched her face and heat flared in my cheeks. I pushed her hand away. There was worse to come. 'The Consecrates forced me to the floor as Sister Merce took a flat wooden paddle from another fold in her habit. She held it out to Sister Constance. You see, I wasn't the only one being taught a lesson that night.'

'I looked around the circle of girls; none of them would meet my eyes. I looked at the Sisters, thinking one of them would step in to stop this, but no. Then I looked at Sister Constance and I remember thinking: *Wasn't corporal punishment outlawed years ago? Isn't this the twenty-first century? Aren't there laws against this?* But this is St Mary's and the rules of the real world don't apply here. I realised that when Sister Constance began to hum as she raised—'

My voice cracked and I covered my face with my hands as the tears came, harder and more painful than on any night since that terrible night.

'Easy Faith, it's okay,' Hope said. I heard her shuffle across the floor as she moved to sit beside me. Her arm slid around my shoulder and, at that moment, we became friends.

'I've kept a low profile ever since,' I said, when my tears slowed. 'I couldn't risk going through that again.'

'I understand.'

'But I've kept my eyes open and I know about them, know what they do here, know what they are.'

Hope raised her eyebrows. 'What are they?'

'Evil,' I replied, and we flinched as, somewhere in the night, a crow screamed.

Chapter Seven

'*Veritas vos Liberabit*,' Hope murmured.

I frowned. They were the first words either of us had said in a few minutes, lost as we were in our thoughts. 'What does that mean?' I asked, wondering how much stranger our conversation was going to get before we returned to the dormitory.

'It's Latin—'

I held up my hand to silence her and concentrated on the room below our feet, listening for any stealthy sounds. We'd been in the attic for about fifteen minutes and I knew we couldn't stay much longer; the Sisters sometimes sprung bed checks, or came for one of the girls.

All was quiet.

I looked at Hope. '—for *the truth will set you free*,' she finished.

'Latin? The dead language?'

'Not as dead as you may think,' Hope replied, and I was taken by a sudden memory of a book I'd read the year before coming to St Mary's.

It wasn't my usual kind of book but I was desperate for something to relieve the boredom while I waited for my mother's weekly Reiki session to end. I'd already read all of the magazine and pamphlets – *Reiki For Beginners*, snore! – in the waiting room over the previous two weeks. I eyed a small bookcase in the corner, not holding out much hope since most of the titles sounded like instruments of torture: *Activate Your Chakra; Whole Body Healing; Devouring the Goddess*, yikes!

One book caught my attention, though: *The Handmaid's Tale*. I took it off the shelf and sat in the bamboo chair under the window, not really expecting much. Three quarters of an hour later, I heard my mother coming down the hallway. *Not yet*, I thought, trying to focus as she paid her account.

'Time to go, sweetheart,' she said, sugar-sweet from her session with the Reiki master.

I ignored her and kept reading about the main character, Offred, and these women she called "walking wombs", who were guarded by the fanatical Aunts.

'Heather. Time to go,' my mother said, an edge slipping into her tone.

The Reiki master touched her elbow. 'Perhaps Heather would like to take the book with her and return it on your next visit?'

'Oh no, we couldn't—'

'Really? Cool, thanks,' I said, using a pamphlet to keep my place in the book.

Two nights later, I finished Offred's story and vowed never to take for granted the rights that shaped my days, and never to let a male dictate the path of my life. I would stand strong. I would heed the message – *Nolite te bastardes Carborundorum* – that Offred found scratched inside her bedroom cupboard: I would never let the bastards grind me down. Of course, said vow only lasted until the end of the week when I fell deeply in lust with Chris Harris: damn it, boys can be *so* distracting.

Now, sitting in the attic at St Mary's, the book came back to me with the force of a summer gale, sweeping aside the curtains across my mind: How different were the Sisters to the Aunts in Offred's world? How many rights did I have now? There were no males here to control my life but weren't the Sisters just as bad? Or worse? Where was their compassion for me? They were female, like me; where was their sense of sisterhood?

'Hey?' Hope touched my arm. '*Veritas vos Liberabit?*'

I held her gaze as I struggled against the storm of thoughts in my head; they couldn't help me, but I had a feeling the girl sitting across from me could, if I'd judged her right. 'The truth? Is that what you're offering?'

Hope's shrugged. 'Sure.'

'Okay, what's with the Latin?'

'It's a little skill I have,' she said, her fingers playing with the edge of her nightgown.

I tried to read the expression on her face but she kept her eyes downcast. 'Was that Latin you used with Sister Merce in her office?'

'Yeah. It seemed appropriate.'

'Why?'

'Because of what she said to me in the dormitory,' Hope replied and lifted her head defiantly. 'She thought she'd freak me out with her mumbo-jumbo, except it's less effective when the person knows what you're saying.' She chuckled but I thought the laugh was a little forced.

'What did she say?'

'*Inter spem et metum gravira manent.* Between hope and fear, greater danger awaits.'

I frowned. 'And what does *that* mean? And why would she say that to you when you've only been here, for what? Five minutes?' I leaned towards her, drawn by the mystery, and looked hard into her face. 'What is it about you that she finds so threatening?'

'Well, I know Latin for a start,' she said.

Good point.

I thought for a moment, remembering the way the nun had scrutinised Hope earlier in the night. 'What did you say to Sister Merce when we were in her office?'

'I told her I was here for the greater glory of God.'

'Oh. And *is* that why you're here?'

Hope's fingers pulled at her nightdress again. 'Maybe. I don't really know, yet. Maybe it has nothing to do with God, or maybe it does. I only know that sometimes we're lead to unexpected places where we're called to do things we never dreamed.' She looked at me to see if I understood the significance of what she was saying, and then turned away as though dissatisfied.

I felt a stab of concern and decided to change the subject. 'So, you know how I ended up here. What about you? What got you thrown into St Mary's?'

Hope tilted her head from side to side, as though weighing up where to begin, or what story to tell, then said, 'The path that brought me here started with a boy. His name was Caleb, he called me his Dao-girl – the girl of the Way – and I loved him, but sometimes loving someone, even if it's with every breath in your body, isn't enough to keep things together.'

I heard the sadness in her voice and touched her arm. 'You don't have to talk about it.'

'It's okay. I need to tell you so you'll understand what's coming.' She saw the question on my face and waved it away. 'Caleb was addicted to heroin, and a junkie wasn't on my mama's list of what she called "acceptable suitors". Of course, I didn't know he was a junkie at first. I thought he was this sweet guy, kind of shy and cute in that Jarred Leto way.'

'Really? Leto's hot.'

'You understand the attraction,' she said, smiling. 'Funny thing, I met Caleb at the movies. He was with a couple of mates and I was with a girlfriend. We'd gone to see some horror film that was so crap we walked out halfway through.

"Was it bad for you too?" he asked as Beth and I strolled past.

"So bad I don't even want a cigarette," I said, and winked at him.

He laughed, getting my joke (his mates gave me a vacant look that should've clued me in, but I just thought they were stupid). "Maybe a Coke would put things right?" he suggested. How could I refuse?

'Beth left after the first Coke and his mates bailed after the second but we sat and talked until Mama rang to find out when I was coming home. After the third call and an earful of threats, I thought I should go. He walked me to the bus stop and waited until the 903 turned the corner, then he kissed me and was gone.

'The next couple of months were bliss. We hung out every chance we got and when we weren't together, we'd be online. He was so cool, and funny, and the best damn kisser.'

A wistful smile touched Hope's lips. I felt a strange twist of emotion; a combination of sympathy and envy. I'd never been that close to a boy but it was definitely on my 'to-do' list (if I ever got out of St Mary's). 'He sounds like a special guy,' I said, hoping she'd tell me more.

'Yeah, I thought so,' Hope said. 'Until the principal of my school called Mama to tell her I'd been ditching class...'

'Ah-huh, not a smart move,' I said.

'I know but I couldn't help it. I wanted to be with him so much. Anyway, the ditching wasn't the problem. It was the "Your daughter is associating with a boy who is a known drug addict" that really fucked things up for

71

us.'

'No way.'

'That's what I said to Mama when she cornered me about it after school. "Caleb doesn't do drugs," I told her, ready to defend him to the death. "He's a beautiful person and I love him."'

'What did she say?' I asked.

'She told me to stop being a drama queen and that I didn't know what love was,' Hope replied. 'Then she said, "It ends today Amy, or else."'

'What did you say?'

'I said, "Or else what? What the fuck are you going to do?" And that's when she slapped my face.'

'Oh my God. What did you do?'

'I got the fuck outta there,' Hope said.

'And went to Caleb's, right?'

Hope blew out a breath. 'Predictable, huh?'

I felt a stab of guilt, as though I'd belittled her somehow. 'No, it's what I would've done.'

'Yeah, and it should've been all good except it wasn't Caleb who answered the door.'

'Who was it?'

'Some drugged-out freak that looked like Caleb, but wasn't the boy I knew. He blinked at me, real slow, you know, like he was trying to focus. "Amy?" he said. It came out slurred and I wanted to smash him right in the face,' Hope said.

I bit my lip; there was an undercurrent of violence rising from the girl beside me that left me shaking. *What sort of ally have I made?* I wondered. 'Did he help you?'

'He couldn't help himself, he was that wasted. Besides, I didn't give him the chance. I bolted. Went back home, snuck up to my room and got into bed. By then, I just wanted the darkness.' Hope sighed and I wondered how I could ease her pain. Then she spoke again and I realised things were about to get weird. 'In the darkness is when the dreams come.'

'Everybody dreams,' I said.

'Not like me. My dreams are prophetic.'

'Really?' I said, trying to keep my voice neutral.

'Hmm, I don't remember much of the dreams, just fragments: Caleb, crows, a room full of shrouded bodies, and the girl with eyes like the ocean.'

'Who's she?'

'She'— another story. Well not really, she's this story but a different part of it.' Her eyes slipped away, searching the floor around her toes.

'It's alright. You don't have to tell me about her.'

'Cool, 'cause she's not important right now.'

Something in her tone suggested she was lying. 'Sure,' I said, and changed the subject. 'So what happened with Caleb?'

'He came by the next day after Mama left for work. She'd given me the "Don't let me down," talk and I fully intended to do what she asked. But when I opened the door, he was standing there with this lame-arsed daisy in his hand, looking so damn sweet—'

'You couldn't resist?'

'We were in my room when Mama found us half an hour later.'

'Crap!'

Hope got to her feet and stretched. 'That's an understatement. Mama went ballistic. "'I know the place for girls like you," she said. And a week later, here I am.'

'And Caleb? Have you seen him since?'

'Only in my dreams.'

'Oh,' I said, unable to keep the sadness out of my voice.

'No, you don't understand. It's okay. I know we'll be together again, it's our destiny. The girl in my dreams told me.'

This time my curiosity got the better of me. 'What else has she told you?' As soon as the words were out, I wanted to take them back; nobody likes a pushy friend.

Hope didn't seem to mind. 'She said there's something in that building next door.' She pointed towards the window.

'You mean the gymnasium?'

'Hmm,' Hope replied as she walked across the beams, her arms held out for balance. 'She said this thing will answer our questions and show us what we're supposed to do next.'

Our? Us?

I grabbed her arm as she reached the stairs. 'I don't follow—'

'Doesn't matter. For now, just trust me, my dreams are never wrong. Come on, we have to get back to the dorm.'

My heart leapt; she was right, we'd been in the attic way too long.

Chapter Eight

Physical activity for the sake of fun or competition was unheard of at St Mary's. The Sisters believed in hard work and discipline but only so they could force us back to 'the narrow path of God's good grace'. That meant sport of any kind – 'an unseemly activity for chaste young women,' so Sister Merce claimed – was prohibited. It also meant they could control our contact with the outside world.

Of course, the Sisters couldn't advertise the lack of sport in their glossy brochure. In a world where youth and fitness are essential, no parent in their right mind would send their kid to a school that had no physical fitness regime, which is why we had 'The Forest'.

St Mary's sat on twenty acres of land, with the school and its buildings – church, convent, church, dorm, and gymnasium – set on five manicured acres along the eastern fence line. Surrounding the school was a dense tract of forest, complete with a small lake and half a dozen walking tracks. According to the Sisters sales pitch, the girls of St Mary's spent two days a week in the forest, hiking, swimming, orienteering, and camping as they learnt life skills such as resilience and leadership. In truth, no girl would voluntarily go into the forest with the Sisters; not – so the rumour went – if she wanted to come out the same girl as she went in.

We still needed to keep fit, though, so Sister Patrice devised a routine that we performed every morning before breakfast: sit ups, push-ups, squats, star jumps. Sometimes I felt I was living in one of those B grade movies where prisoners, dressed in grey uniforms, jump up and down like robots while their overseers yell abuse at them. The tragedy was it wasn't too far from our reality.

On top of the prison-camp exercise regime, there were the repetitive duties like polishing floors and scrubbing windows. Boring as these chores were, at least, they kept us out of the Sister's way, and that was a blessing no matter how much I hated doing them.

As Hope and I stood outside the gymnasium, the irony of our punishment wasn't lost on me. In the long months of my confinement, I'd never seen a girl even enter the gym, let alone play sport there. Now we were expected to clean it from top to bottom.

Excellent.

My stomach rumbled. It'd been almost three hours since we'd climbed from our beds and forced down a tasteless breakfast before sitting through a dreary sixty-minute lecture on Benevolence. *Our cup runneth over with irony this morning*, I thought, as I reached for the door handle.

'Wait,' Hope said, grabbing my hand.

'What?' I glanced over my shoulder, expecting to see a nun bearing down on us but the pathway was empty. I looked back at Hope. 'What's up?'

In reply, Hope placed her hands against the bricks. She closed her eyes as her fingers explored the wall, delving into the cracks and crevices. Her head was turned to the side as though she was listening, and her lips moved.

'Umm, what are you doing?' I asked.

'Discovering,' she replied, opening her eyes.

Right.

'That's really interesting and all, but if we don't get started on this,' I waved the list I was holding at her, 'we'll never get everything finished by the afternoon.'

'Stop worrying,' Hope said, taking my hand and placing it on the bricks. 'Tell me what you feel.'

'Nothing,' I said.

Hope pressed her hand over mine. 'Try.'

I closed my eyes, concentrating on the cool roughness pricking my palm. Soon I felt it: a vibration, strong and rhythmic like the thrum of a machine. 'What *is* that?' I whispered.

'History,' Hope replied, reaching for the door.

It was dark inside and our heavy shoes sent echoes rolling as though we'd entered a vast underground cavern. The air was stale and a sneeze burst from me. Hope laughed as she felt around for the lights and flicked the switch. Overhead, three of the seven bulbs flared into life. Rows of windows, perched over the bleachers and lining the long wall, did little to relieve the gloom since their panes were coated in a layer of grime.

1. All windows to be cleaned, inside and out.

Great.

At each end of the gym were the blank faces of basketball backboards, staring at each other across the dull wooden floor like time-forgotten giants. Lines in yellow and white crisscrossed the court, while halfway down and piled to the side, were poles and netting for volleyball. On the far wall hung rows of rackets; tennis, squash, badminton, their heads limp and unsprung.

2. Floors to be swept, scrubbed and polished.

Awesome.

'Why do they have this stuff if we never get to use it? I wondered aloud.

'To keep up appearances,' Hope replied as she walked deeper into the gymnasium, turning at random and sometimes stopping as though her way was blocked.

I followed her with my eyes. Her movements confused me and I didn't like the weird expression on her face, which was sort of dreamy and distant like she wasn't really in the same place as me. I didn't want her to see my discomfort so I hid my feelings in exploration. On my left was a small room with a shuttered window; the canteen, I guessed. Rusted hinges squealed as I pushed open the door and turned on the light, sending a battalion of cockroaches scattering. I shivered with disgust.

In the centre of the room was a Formica table. An old fridge, its enamel yellow as a nicotine stain, stood in one corner. A chrome sink and a dusty bain marie lined the far wall.

3. Kitchen: clean cupboards, polish utensils and equipment.

Sweet.

How ordinary the kitchen seemed, but when I tried to imagine Sister Assumpta serving a line of chattering, starving girls their post-game fix of Cokes and hot chips, I couldn't do it. The Sisters were many things, but ordinary wasn't one of them. I wandered out, leaving the light on; we'd be back soon enough.

Hope wasn't in the gym. I glanced at the front door, which was closed, and then followed her winding footprints through the dust to a room at the far end of the hall. I stood inside the doorway, waiting for my eyes to adjust to the gloom. To my left were the toilet cubicles. Opposite them, basins were lined up against the wall like criminals.

But no Hope.

I looked to the right; two rows of metal lockers

stood at attention. I stepped further into the room and checked for Hope between the lockers, but she seemed to have vanished. *Did she go outside?* I wondered.

Ahead of me was another doorway, through which came a soft scrape and the pattering of something hard falling onto the floor. I approached slowly. It was darker inside the room and I could just make out the shower cubicles.

4. Toilets, showers, basins and lockers to be scrubbed and disinfected.

My life's ambition.

The pattering came again. I frowned. This time there was a sly quality to the sound, as though someone was trying to conceal their activities. It had to be Hope; who else could it be? But as I strained to see, I realised I was far from certain that it *was* Hope.

There was something about the room that made me nervous; a rising heat, which touched me like a powerful memory. I wanted to step inside, to cross the threshold but, at the same time, I was unsure.

What would I change by taking that step?

Doubt gripped me; was my life at St Mary's really that bad? I had a bed and three meals a day and enough to keep me busy so I was never bored. Yeah okay, maybe that meant longer school days than kids on 'the outside', followed by hours of monotonous study and prayer, broken up by mind-numbing chores, and the unending task of avoiding the Sisters and the Consecrates, but it was okay. Wasn't it? Sure. If I discounted the screams in the night and the way girls sometimes disappeared. I resisted for another second, until Hope whispered my name.

The quality of the light changed as soon as I crossed the threshold; everything was in sepia shades, like an old-fashioned photograph. I stepped deeper into the gloom, taking in the bench seats lining the walls and the long mottled mirror to my right that captured the entire room.

The gentle pattering came again and I started to turn, but something in the mirror caught my eye. The glass shimmered and the image caught in its reflection wavered; changed. Instead of showers and bench seats, two long tables appeared in the centre of the room, while against the wall were cupboards filled with old-fashioned irons and rows of heating stones. Looking back through the door reflected in the mirror, I could see cast-iron washing tubs and something that looked like a cement mixer stuffed with sheets. I moved closer and pressed my hand to the slick surface of the mirror. When I pulled my fingers away, they were moist. I swept my hand across the glass, knowing it would have no effect; the images were embedded memories.

As the mirror steamed over again, I saw Hope caught in its reflection. She was kneeling beside a cupboard against the far wall, her hands working at something in front of her. I spun around and, as I did, the vision in the mirror disappeared.

'Hope?'

She looked at me. 'It's here,' she said.

'What is?' I asked, coming up behind her.

'The thing the girl in my dream said we need,' she replied, digging away at the mortar between the bricks. There was a small pile of rubble between her feet. 'Can't you feel it?' The muscles flexed beneath her blouse as she pulled at a brick, which moved like a loose tooth not yet ready to give up the comfort of its socket. She slipped her fingers into the gap around the brick and worked on the mortar.

I closed my eyes and tried to sense the thing she was seeking, and for a moment, it was there: a voice, soft and sweet. The sound sent tingles along my spine. I bent down next to Hope and scraped away the mortar around the brick beside the one she was working on, ignoring the sandpaper roughness that shredded the pads of my fingertips. The brick slid towards me. At the same time, Hope yanked at her own brick and toppled onto her backside as it came loose. I sat back next to Hope, who was peering into the opening we'd created in the wall.

Her breathing was loud, filling the room. She dropped the brick and dipped her hand into the blackness. Her eyes narrowed and a smile curved her mouth as she drew an object out of the hole, moving with a terrible slow reverence as she brought it into the twenty-first century.

Chapter Nine

Curiosity is good, but it should be tempered by a healthy dose of survival instinct.

I don't remember where I read this snippet of advice – probably in one of my mum's *Cleo* or *Cosmo* magazines – but, standing in that shower recess, I couldn't have agreed more. As Hope gazed at the book, which was grey with dust and bulging in places where moisture had worked under its cover, an uncomfortable certainty crept over me: we had to get out of that room.

I took Hope by the elbow and pulled her towards the exit. 'We need more light,' I said, in case she resisted, but she was also eager to leave the bathroom. We entered the gym and sat on the floor beneath one of the overhead lamps. Hope placed the book between us and, in the yellow light, I could see it was a diary. The leather cover was maroon with four rust-tarnished clips at each corner. There was no inscription on the front. The pages were stuck together in layered clumps and I wondered how we were going to read them.

Hope frowned. She poked at the pages and ran her finger along the book's spine. 'I don't know if we'll be able to read it,' she said, as though she'd pulled the thought from my mind, but then I realised it wasn't the condition of the book that worried her. She glanced at me and I saw reluctance in her eyes. I thought back to the moment before I had crossed the threshold into the showers: how would this change everything?

Hope placed her hand over the diary, her fingers spread. 'I believe this holds the secrets of the Sisterhood,' she said.

I drew a quick breath. In the excitement of our discovery, I had forgotten the Sisters and what we were supposed to be doing in the gymnasium. A sense of urgency ploughed into me and I knew without doubt that Sister Assumpta was on her way to the gymnasium to check on us. I grabbed the diary, ignoring Hope's yell of protest, and raced over to the bleachers. When I found a reasonable hiding place, I pushed the diary inside.

Hope was behind me, grabbing for my arm. 'What are you doing?' she demanded.

I took her hand and pulled her towards the kitchen. 'Trust me,' I said, as I opened a cupboard and began emptying its contents. Under the sink I found rags and unused cleaning products. I grabbed some polish and shoved it in Hope's hand. She stared at the bottle and then at me as though I'd lost my mind. 'Use it,' I said as I squirted cleaner across the closest bench top and scrubbed, finding the elbow grease my mother always said I lacked.

As I swished water across the sink, I looked up to find Sister Assumpta glowering at us from the doorway. 'You girls have been in here for half an hour. Is this all you have managed to accomplish?'

'Sorry Sister. We were working out what needed to be done and where we should start,' I said, praying Hope would keep her mouth shut. 'There's just so much to do.' I let a whiny note creep into my voice, knowing it would make Sister Assumpta's skin crawl. It was a risk; if she was feeling spiteful she would turn on us like a cornered feral cat and make the punishment a thousand times worse, but if she was feeling magnanimous, she would make a hasty retreat before we could sour her mood.

'Just get a move on. You don't have all week to complete that list,' she said, before stomping out of the gym.

Hope dropped the cloth on the table. As she headed for the kitchen door, she asked, 'How did you know she was coming?'

'Don't know,' I said, following her back to the bleachers. 'A little voice in my head, maybe,' I said drawing the book out and handing it to Hope. We climbed to the top row of seats and sat beneath a window.

'I've dreamed this moment,' Hope said.

'Really? When?'

'The night before I came here.'

I frowned as a question surfaced in my mind, but Hope peeled the book open and my attention was captured. On the first page was an inscription written in a sweeping cursive; five lines of a dedication blurred with age and moisture. Only the name was legible.

'Jennifer,' I whispered. There were a few words that I could just make out: *one, love, together* and *promise*. I sighed at the romance in them.

Hope flicked through the pages until she came to a name we both recognised: *Sister Merce*.

The shock hit me like a fist. I shook my head. 'It couldn't be,' I said.

Hope remained silent and returned to the first page. She pointed to the date at the top: 3rd April 1909.

'What's the date today?' she asked.

My silence was her answer.

'A hundred and ten years,' Hope said, as though it was what she expected, and I wondered again who she was and how she had come to be at St Mary's.

Hope glanced at me and closed the diary. She took a moment to think and then said, 'I know you have lots of questions and I'll try to answer them, but there's some stuff I don't know yet and other stuff I don't have time to explain.' She stood. 'I'll tell you what I can, but let's work while I do. No point giving the Sisters more reason to punish us.'

I nodded. 'Kitchen?'

'Fabulous,' Hope said, clasped the diary to her chest in mock excitement.

The laughter that burst out of me was a surprise and I clapped a hand over my mouth to stifle it, afraid the Sisters would hear.

Hope drew my hand away. 'It's okay to laugh,' she said.

'No, it's not. Not here.'

'Laughter is more important here than anywhere, even if you only hold it in your heart. Don't let them steal it from you.' She looked at me steadily for a second then crossed her eyes and puffed out her cheeks. 'Wow, look who's got their Zen on,' she said, and we laughed as we entered the kitchen and took up our discarded cloths.

Hope moved with purpose now and I followed her lead as I listened. 'I told you that I sometimes know stuff, remember? Like the Latin?' She asked the question but didn't look at me for a response. 'And I told you I have dreams. Sometimes they'll be about someone I know or about something that's going to happen. Not always serious stuff, like the time I dreamt my cousin, Suzie, would meet Aaron, the guy she married. But some are different, full of symbols and hard to decipher. Those are the dreams I take notice of because they're usually important.'

She turned to the fridge. The shelving rattled as she opened the door. A grimace clouded her face at the musty electrical smell that wafted through the kitchen.

'Was the dream about the girl with eyes like the ocean one of the important ones?' I asked.

Hope turned from the fridge and gazed at me until I began to worry that I'd asked the wrong thing.

Stupid.

Then she nodded and said, 'Yeah. Very important.' She raised her eyebrows. 'The diary, remember?'

'Oh yeah, I know. I just thought maybe there was something else.'

'You're a perceptive one, aren't you?' she said, and I felt a flush of pride. She smiled and went on. 'The girl started coming to me just before I met Caleb. In my dreams, she always appeared in a swirling mist. Her eyes were sad and she held her hands beneath her chin, as though she was praying for me. I tried to talk to her but she would turn away. This went on for a few weeks until one night I dreamt she came and sat at the foot of my bed, and I knew she was ready to speak.'

'Does it freak you out?'

'What?'

'The dreams and stuff?'

'Nah. It's always been like that so I'm used to it.'

'I'd be freaked out,' I said.

'I don't know about that. Maybe you're stronger than you think.'

I shrugged, not wanting to disagree with her but knowing I wasn't anywhere near as strong as she assumed. 'So what did the girl say?'

Hope gazed at me for a few seconds before saying, 'She said there was an ancient force at work that must be stopped, but they couldn't do it alone; they needed me and one other.'

Hope pointed towards me and a strange feeling

pulled at my stomach as though I was in the grip of something I couldn't refuse. 'Who are "they"?' I asked.

'The girl with eyes like the ocean is one,' Hope said, tapping the diary. 'Jennifer. Or Grace, as the Sisters called her in her time.'

'What Sisters?' I asked, already knowing the answer but not willing to believe it.

Hope nodded in the direction of the convent as though that was all she needed to say on the matter. 'Grace needs my help. Our help. I don't know who else, yet. Not that it matters. Everything in my life has been moving towards this moment, preparing me for what's ahead. The voices in my head, the dreams, Caleb, meeting you, even this stupid punishment.'

I stared at her. *The voices?*

She closed the fridge door. 'It's all been a part of it.'

'A part of what?' I asked.

She lifted her shoulders. 'We'll find out when we read the diary.'

Part Two

The Book of Grace and Charity

The Citadel of Reminiscence

Return
Not to the House of Doors,
Its vaulted corridor,
Meandering.
In the room of echoes,
The forgotten season,
Languishing.
Venture
Not To the Palace of Memory,
Wherein awaits,
The alluring chalice,
Of antiquity's grievance,
Of ancient triumphs.
Taste
Not the wine of aridity,
Dust in thy mouth,
Seek with eyes blind,
Witness the fall of Grace,
The lie of time,
Upon the crumbling hearth,
The tarnished crown of
Entropy.

Page One

3rd April 1909.

Oh precious gift, where should I begin? Perhaps with the miracle that happened today. A miracle that began with a simple word: a name.

My name.

My real name.

Jennifer.

How I tremble as I remember this wondrous morning. The air was brisk and clear, and the first baskets of washing for the day crowded around my legs like timid children as I lifted the sheets onto the clothesline. The Sisters take in laundry from the local hotels and lodging houses, which they force us – the Fallen – to wash and iron as punishment for our wickedness; for the unforgivable sin of being female.

My fingers stung as I tugged at the cold sheets, conscious of the Sister's insistence on precision in everything we do: *God is perfection. Reflect this in every undertaking and you will be closer to returning to his loving embrace.* At that moment, however, God's embrace was a distant concern.

Jennifer?

I grew still: *Could it be him?*

Impossible.

I shook my head. It seemed my mind had finally succumbed to the torments of this place. Still, I peered between the sheets, hoping against hope, even as my mind murmured that it was the Sisters playing a trick on me, such small cruelties being their milk and honey.

There was no one to be seen beyond the sheets. I was alone. A crow in the nearby Poinciana released a mournful cry and I sighed: dreams and wishes.

Jennifer!

There was no mistake this time. My heart pounded. It was Patrick, the boy I dared to love and the reason I am here, watched over by the Sisterhood – the savage protectors of my virtue.

As I dragged aside the sheet and searched the ivy-covered wall that surrounded the convent, I was re-minded of Joan of Arc and how she heard the voice of God commanding her to do His will. Although I would never presume to compare our love to the experience of Joan (for to do so would be the blackest blasphemy), I can imagine the joy and fear she must have felt as God spoke to her, for I felt the same when Patrick spoke to me.

I whispered his name, afraid the Sisters would hear me, even from the convent. There is good reason for my fear, as I have witnessed their frightful, uncanny instincts. Patrick's laughing reply, however, left me in no doubt of his identity.

No Jenny, it's the Pope. I've come to absolve you of your sins so they'll let you out of this prison.

Mind your tongue and manners, Patrick McManning.

He laughed again and bade me come to the corner of the wall. As I reached the spot, Patrick's hand shot through the ivy and grabbed my arm. I let out a yelp and pulled away even as Patrick gently shushed me. My nerves fluttered as I twisted the ivy aside to find Pat-rick's face framed by a rough-edged square cut into the stone.

How do I describe the joy I felt at seeing him after all these months? When I think about that first moment, all I can remember is the love that shone in his eyes as he smiled at me. Everything else disappeared: the convent, the Sisters, the laundry, the hurt and terror, and it was just us, together again.

I cried and Patrick stroked my wrist, murmuring for me to be brave as he was trying to secure my freedom. Hope washed over me at his words. However, it was soon dashed as he confessed that his approaches to our parish priest had come to naught.

But don't worry, my lovely girl, I will find a way to rescue you, even if I must climb these walls and spirit you away in the dead of night.

As he spoke, his hand slipped back through the gap in the wall, returning a few seconds later with a package wrapped in plain brown paper. I took it with shaking hands, glancing over my shoulder again. Seeing my mounting disquiet, Patrick instructed me to unwrap the gift quickly, which I did and then gazed in delight at this very diary in which I write. The cover was deep maroon, its edges tipped with gleaming gold clips, and I wondered how he could afford such a thing. Inside, Patrick had written:

My darling Jennifer,
You are the holder of my heart.
Press your love between these pages and know,
We will be together again.
This I promise.
Eternally yours, Patrick

Tears welled in my eyes as I searched for the words to convey what his gift meant to me, but Patrick hushed me with a caution: *Hide it well, sweet heart, and take care until we speak again.* Then he was gone.

Pain as sharp as nettles pricked at my heart, but I could not allow the anguish to conquer me. I slipped the book beneath my skirt. Its weight was a constant reminder of my love as I hurried to finish hanging the washing, aware I had taken far too long already.

As I entered the laundry, Sister Sarah – one of the novices at St Mary's and a true heart – sent me a questioning glance. I deposited the washing baskets beside the last clothes wringer and dropped a curtsy by way of apology as I asked permission to use the lavatory. The nun agreed, with a warning to be hasty. I nodded, keeping my eyes lowered. I had no intention of being otherwise.

The ironing room was on the way to the lavatory. I checked over my shoulder, searching for prying eyes, and slipped into the room. A small prayer of thanks formed on my lips as I approached the far wall. Usually the Sisters were sticklers for perfection but a rare oversight in maintenance had resulted in the deterioration of the brickwork beside the cupboard where the irons were kept.

The loose bricks shifted under my determined fingers and came away with a trickle of dirt. The hole was the perfect size; deep enough to conceal the diary without drawing attention once the bricks were replaced. I brushed the mortar from my hands and turned for the laundry, satisfied the diary was safe until I could get my new treasure to a more secure location.

And here we are diary, in the attic – my sanctuary – and out of harm's way for the moment. Time is short, however, and there is much to write, to purge, but first, a confession. I know as a good Catholic, I should not harbour hatred towards another, yet my heart is a lump of stone where Sister Merce is concerned. Not one ounce of warmth can I muster for her. Nor can I find, in the depth of her eyes, any compassion for me.

It is for this reason that I feel no guilt for the act of theft I committed today.

The opportunity to purloin the treasures I hold in my hands – a fountain pen and ink with which to write in Patrick's diary – came about through an unexpected chance to be alone in Father Michael's church. I'd been sent to collect the linens for laundering when the priest was called away to attend to one of the girls; a call that filled me with dread.

There are three ways danger finds a girl at St Mary's: a problem with her pregnancy, ingesting a lethal dose of bleach – a hideously painful death – or falling afoul of the Sisters. I hoped for the first reason, which at least offered the girl the chance of survival. Still, I tried not to contemplate the fate of the poor wretch too much, for her suffering afforded me a rare opportunity: time unwatched.

I completed my duty with haste and soon found myself wandering the rooms of the church until I came to Father Michael's private quarters. I am not inquisitive by nature but something drew me through his study door and over to the desk under the window. Sunlight fell upon the safety pen and eyedropper lying in their blue velvet case, and I seemed to hear a faraway voice telling me to take the implements.

Whose voice was it? Lucifer's? My conscience? I don't know, and I had no time to think for I saw Father Michael returning to the church, and he was not alone. I gathered up the case and a small bottle of ink sitting beside it, and scrambled into the Sanctuary, looking for somewhere to hide them.

Sister Merce called my name from the doorway of the church – *Grace!* – and I turned, ducking my head as she ordered me back to the laundry. Fear twisted through my stomach as I hurried past her and the priest for, wrapped inside the bundle I carried, was the pen and ink I'd plundered.

My heart thudded until I entered the laundry. When the latch clicked behind me, I breathed a sigh and scurried to the empty ironing room where I hid the fruits of my pilfering beside Patrick's diary before returning to the washing room.

As I toiled beside the other girls, thoughts of the diary plagued my mind. I wanted to be away from the steam and sickly-sweet smell of soap. The book seemed to call to me and I was impatient for the opportunity to sneak away and write on its smooth, fresh pages. The chance came, in the shape of a tragedy, ten minutes before Confession.

One of the penitents, a petulant girl named Anne, was loading sodden sheets into the wringer when I heard her groan. No one paid attention; at almost eight months pregnant, we were used to her moaning and sighing, but when she groaned again, deep and hurting, I had to risk a glance in her direction.

Anne clutched at her swollen belly. Her face blanched and her lips moved, perhaps forming the name of her unborn child, as she collapsed. Convulsions shook her body and she gurgled as though she was drowning inside. I leaned over her, catching the sharp reek of bleach fumes. Understanding filled me and I stared at Anne in horror.

The Sisters flew into the room like a flock of crows. 'All of you, to the dormitory,' Sister Anslem ordered. She shoved me out of the way and took Anne by the shoulders, pinning her to the wet floor. The last thing I saw as I turned for the ironing room was the nun pressing her mouth over Anne's grimacing lips. I ran.

With the Sisters preoccupied, it may be expected

that our routine would descend into chaos, but we are too submissive for that to occur. Instead, we attended Confession and sat silently through dinner, followed by an hour of 'recreation', prayer and finally, bed. We don't dare deviate from the established pattern for the Consecrates, who are the eyes and ears of the Sisterhood, oversee our every move.

Sometimes I wonder which of our keepers is worse.

Through the torturous hours between Anne's collapse and lights out, the fear of discovery haunted me. I'd hidden the diary and writing implements beneath my mattress in the dormitory until I could move them to the attic. Each time a Consecrate left us on some errand, I was sure she would return with the pilfered items. Each time a Consecrate returned empty-handed, I said a prayer of thanks.

My anxiety mounted as I lay in the dark, feeling the pen case and inkbottle pressing into my back, while I waited for the girls to settle for the night. Nor did the feeling ease when their breathing surrendered to the rhythm of sleep. I left my bed and crossed to the linen press at the end of the room, taking tentative steps as though the floor was carpeted with knives.

It was an agonising journey, but being in the attic makes the anxiety worthwhile.

Finding the attic was a blessing orchestrated, I'm sure, by the Lord. Hearing my prayers for a sanctuary from the cruelties of the Sisterhood, He worked in his mysterious way and provided what I needed where I least expected to find it.

I'd been sent from the laundry with a pile of freshly laundered sheets, which were to be stored in the linen press. As I carried these into the cupboard, I stumbled – although to this day, I do not know upon what –

sending the sheets flying in all directions. I dropped to the floor and began gathering the fallen linen, hoping I would not be discovered by the ever-wrathful Sisters. As I piled the sheets, I notice a shaft of weak light coming from the far end of the cupboard. Curious, I crept over to investigate and discovered a door. I searched for a handle and heard a soft snick. The door swung open. Six steps lead to another door partially open, like a divine invitation, at the top of the stairs.

The attic was a mausoleum. Wardrobes filled with moth-eaten habits, trunks with padlocked lids inscribed with Latin, a bookshelf lined with Bibles, crucifixes and tarnished chalices, paintings of Saints hidden under dustcovers, an old wooden pew with a split leg, and a hundred other treasures pushed against the walls. Neglect hung heavy over the room, yet I felt at ease. Perhaps it was the sunlight flowing through the single round window, bathing the religious relics in a soft buttery glow, or that the malevolence permeating St Mary's appeared to be absent. Whatever the reason, I felt sheltered and somehow closer to God in the attic.

This closeness is a blessing but, tonight, it is tarnished by the dark guilt in my heart. I have broken the Eighth Commandment – Thou shalt not steal – and I wonder if God will forgive me, even if I have acted for the higher purpose of documenting the evil that resides within His garden?

And what of Patrick? Would he forgive my deceitful act?

How this question plays on my conscience. Yet, I must release the pent-up frustrations the Sisters have forced upon me; for to keep my feelings inside is to court madness. Would Patrick understand this? I believe he would. Why else would he have shared this gift if not to provide me with a small measure of freedom?

Freedom: such an inconsequential word, or so I

thought until Patrick came into my life.

I remember the day we met as though I had lived it today. My family and I were picnicking with the Andersons at our favourite swimming spot the first time I saw Patrick. Their daughter, Catherine, and I had grown up together and she teased me when she saw me staring at the boy who lounged roguishly upon the grass. I sniffed and told her not to be ridiculous. Yet, my eyes wandered to him and I blushed each time I found him looking at me. Later in the day, when my mother and Mrs Anderson took the younger children to look for crabs along the river's edge, he seized the opportunity to talk to us.

You're a St Margaret's girl, aren't you? He might as well have asked me to marry him right there and then, for at the sound of his voice, I fell in love.

That was in October and by the beginning of December we were spending every moment we could together without raising the suspicions of our families. I still don't understand why our parents frown upon love. I would have thought being in love was a gift from God, but my father made it clear that boys were strictly out-of-bounds.

Patrick's family was equally against love, as was our parish priest, Father O'Donnell, who constantly asserted that only the love between the Faithful and God was acceptable. As such, we kept our love a secret, for (we joked) our fathers would have strung Patrick up by his thumbs if they knew he was courting me and I – oh, cursed irony – would have been banished to a convent. Yet, willing spirits can always find a way, and Patrick and I did all we could to be together.

We met early in the morning and ambled to our respective schools, arriving as the bell sounded. Sister Ruth was not impressed with my last minute dash into her classroom. Nor was she impressed with my rush for the door in the afternoon, but I cared little for her opinion. The only thing on my mind was Patrick.

I met him at the river and, for an hour, we would stroll hand in hand along the bank, talking and discovering each other. For that hour, I felt as though I was made of sunshine. Then, a quarter to five would come and I would have to leave in order to make it home by my five o'clock curfew, but each day it became harder to separate from him, especially when I saw the love in Patrick's eyes.

Weekends were the most difficult time as we were forced to spend two days apart. For me, there were chores around the house and homework and, when that was done, there was 'the Calling'. My parents are pillars of our Church, and for as long as I can remember, my siblings, Lillian and James, and I were expected to be involved in charity work. We visited the sick, read to the elderly and, sometimes, collected alms for the Church. I didn't mind the work as it allowed me to help those in need, but that changed once I met Patrick.

For the first time in my life, impatience blossomed within me. I came to resent playing nursemaid to old ladies when I wanted to daydream about Patrick and what our lives were going to be like when we were married. To get through those long hours of service, I prayed fervently for Monday morning.

In my anticipation of seeing Patrick, I didn't heed the quizzical looks my mother gave me as I floated around the kitchen while she prepared breakfast for the family. Nor did I notice my father's arched eyebrow at the snatch of song I hummed as I straightened the ribbon in my hair and carefully lifted my satchel onto my shoulder so as not to wrinkle my pinafore.

Lillian tried to warn me in her awkward twelve-year-old way. *Why are you acting like such a goose?* she asked one morning as she skipped down our front path behind me. I looked over my shoulder without slowing and told her to leave me alone. She stopped in the middle of the footpath. As I turned the corner out of our street, I saw her face was clouded with concern but I could not attend to her fancies. Time was moving and I knew that if I didn't see Patrick soon, I would surely die.

I must stop here, diary. There is a howling on the wind. The Sisters are finished with Anne.

Page Six

5th April 1909,

Sometimes I wonder at the prescience of Father Michael. As God's servant, how can he not hear the quaver in my voice as I sit in the confessional and lie about my sinfulness? How can he not see in the depths of my eyes the secrets in my heart?

Perhaps it is as my mother says: *The moral see only what is good.*

Is this why I see the evil that pervades the Sisterhood while Father Michael seems oblivious?

Yet, if I am wicked, is this not the fault of the Sisters? It is, after all, their insistence that I am a "fallen woman" and their brutal determination to cleanse me of such a claim that has forced me to such a deceitful act. If only they would allow us some freedom, perhaps I could be saved from my sins, and the terror of discovery each time the wind shrieks through the eaves above the attic.

The last time my heart beat this wildly was on the day I stayed an extra ten minutes with Patrick at the river and arrived home late to find my father waiting for me on our front veranda. As a small child, a simple frown from my father was enough to reduce me to tears. Walking up to him, I saw his stern expression and felt my eyes begin to sting. I blinked and reminded myself that I had my excuse ready.

'Sorry I'm late, Father,' I said, lowering my eyes. 'I was at the library and lost track of the time.'

My father remained silent and I stole a look at his face, which remained stony. Seeing this, I knew something more than my tardiness was wrong. My mother appeared at the front door, her eyes red-rimmed as she murmured something about the neighbours. My father gave a derisive grunt and came down the stairs. I back peddled but it was too late. He grasped my arm and pulled me into the house, dragging me past my subdued brother and sister, down to the kitchen, where he deposited me on a chair at the table and sat opposite. My mother stood behind him, her allegiance clear.

I kept my eyes lower. *All this because I was ten minutes late?* I wondered, feeling a twist of bewilderment. This was not the first time I'd been late home. Indeed, sometimes when Lillian, James and I were out on the Calling—

Then my father said Patrick's name.

My head jerked up and I stared at my parents, not knowing what to say.

I was my father's favourite child. In all of my sixteen years, he had never raised his voice to me, though I had often seen him angry with Lillian or James, but now he looked upon me with anger etched deep into his face and said the only thing I never wanted to hear.

'I forbid you to see that boy again.'

Something shifted within me, heaving a word up from the pit of my stomach and forcing it from my mouth. 'No!'

Even without the shock on my father's face and the hand that fluttered to my mother's lips, I knew I had overstepped a boundary. I braced myself for my father's wrath.

He shoved his chair away from the table and I shrank away, terrified. His hand moved and I waited for him to remove his belt, sure I was about to receive the first beating of my life. Instead, he took my mother by her elbow as he looked down on me.

'So be it,' he said, his voice so cold it raised gooseflesh across my arms. Without another word or backward glance, he led my mother out of the kitchen.

Did I regret my defiance? Not in the quarter hour I remained alone, wondering desperately what was happening to Patrick. Did his parents know about us? I thought it probable. My father always went to the heart of any problem, which meant he would have spoken to Patrick's parents the moment he knew of our relationship. Was Patrick, even then, on the receiving end of a beating meted out by his father, a man renowned for his temper? I was out of the kitchen and down the back stairs before I had time to consider the consequences of what I was doing.

Three streets from his house, I ran into Patrick.

At first, I didn't recognise him and I struggled to break free of the arms that held me, until he spoke my name. My heart soared and I threw myself against him. He grunted and I pulled away. His lips were swollen and there was a bruise developing beneath his eye. I reached to touch his face but Patrick took my hand and led me across the street, under the fringe of a willow tree, where he kissed me for the first time. His mouth was soft and warm, yet salty from the blood that flecked his lips. I pressed hard against him, hoping the kiss would last forever, but we were torn from each other.

I was dragged to a covered sulky and hoisted onto the seat. I turned, ready to leap back into the mêlée that had erupted with Patrick at its centre, but a hand, cold and insistent, gripped my wrist, making me cry out and turn. Beside me, a figure shifted and the white face of a nun peered at me.

'Let go,' I cried, and gasped as my mother's hand struck me across the cheek. She was sitting on the opposite seat and I hadn't noticed her in my shock. The nun tutted, admonishing my mother for her violence. For a moment, I thought I had an ally in the Sister, but one look into her ghastly face was enough to convince me otherwise.

A shout from beyond the carriage returned my attention to Patrick. He was standing between four men: our fathers and our parish priests. His dad held him by the back of his neck and every now and then, he shook him, causing Patrick's arms to flop in a frightful way. I wanted to run to him, to rescue him, but the nun held me in place, her hand a vice.

The men around Patrick conferred heatedly before Father O'Donnell and my father broke away and strode towards us. Their faces were set with a horrible determination as they stepped into the carriage, taking a seat beside my mother and the nun.

Patrick was dragged towards a second carriage. As he stumbled up the step, he turned and searched until his eyes found mine. I leaned forward, ignoring the adults, and watched his lips.

'I love you,' he said, before his father pushed him inside. Hands pressed me against the seat but I didn't care. Patrick loved me and there was nothing on God's earth that could take that away.

How right and yet, how wrong I was about that, although I understood little about these things on the night Patrick and I were separated. All I knew then was that the carriage in which I was being held captive was travelling in the opposite direction to my home, to a destination unknown to me. Illumination was provided by Father O'Donnell as he patted my mother's hand to ease her weeping.

'Be at peace, my dear. Sister Merce and the Sisters of *Maria De Los Delores* will take good care of our lost child,' he said. I glanced at the nun as I translated the name: *Mary of the Suffering*. A twinge of unease plucked at my heart. Sister Merce was smiling.

My unease turned to outright fear when Father O'Donnell launched into a sermon that made the reason for my confinement clear. According to him, I had sinned. Yet, as I listened to the priest who had baptised me, I struggled to understand how I'd been transformed into a sinner who needed saving from my "wicked desires and uncontrollable lusts" – my apparently traitorous female nature.

I shook my head in the darkness. Who was this person of whom Father O'Donnell spoke? Not me, surely? I was good, wasn't I? I went to Church and said my prayers every night; I did charity work and sang in the choir. I loved Patrick, yes, but I wasn't a sinner. Yet they – the adults who claimed to know me best – looked upon me as though the stain of my corruption was as evident as the stigmata.

I could see the same accusation in the eyes of the nuns as Sister Merce led me through the convent and up the stairs to a vacant bed in the dormitory.

This evening we have the pleasure of welcoming a new initiate. Girls, this is Grace. She will be with us for a long while, so teach her the rules and ensure she remains true to God's Path.

I stared at her. *Grace?*

Confusion and despair overwhelmed me as I thought of all I had lost in a few short hours – the love of my life, my family, my home and now, my name. Was there no end to this nightmare?

Those first few lonely weeks were filled with tears

and sleeplessness; with hours spent kneeling in silent prayer; with unexplained cries of terror in the night. Somehow, I survived and learnt the routine:

Rise at four-thirty.

Mass in the Chapel at quarter to five.

Breakfast at six, followed by work in the laundry until half twelve.

Lunch.

An hour of prayer until two of the clock.

Return to the laundries until half past five.

Confession.

Dinner at six o'clock, followed by more reflection and more prayers until eight. Lights out at half past eight.

The routine is dull beyond description, and the only change we experience is in the amount of work the Sister's force upon us. Mondays are the worst. It is then that the linens from the local hotels and inns are delivered: bag after bag of sheets, pillowcases, tablecloths and towels that must be washed, dried, ironed and folded ready to be picked up on Tuesday morning. There's no rest for us that day, not even for those penitents – like poor Anne and her cousin, Bernadette, who is also heavy with child – who need it most.

I feel my own exhaustion as I write this and there will be a debt of weariness to pay tomorrow, so I must end here for tonight. More importantly, I can see them scurrying across the moonlit lawns, hastening about their hideous business. They don't fear discovery, for all who live behind these walls are mute with terror and those beyond the walls are blind to the truth, so clever is their disguise.

How is it that our Father in Heaven suffers such creatures to exist? I have prayed for an answer to this question, but God remains silent on the matter.

Page Nineteen

15th April 1909.

What is it about females that makes the world so hostile to us? What does the world fear? And what of our complicity in the betrayal of our sex, despite the common abilities and nature we share? Why do women separate from each other and to what purpose? Whom does this separation serve, for surely it is not us?

I have no answers to these questions but, if there is a lesson to learn from my time in this crucible of sinful females, it is that we are our own worst enemies and, at the same time, our most proficient keepers. Yet, there may be one "fallen" female with the temerity to revolt against this deplorable division; a slip of a girl whom has caught my attention.

The Sisters named her Charity.

On the day Bernadette gave birth, Charity and I had been assigned to the sewing room, which was a veritable paradise compared to the steamy washing rooms where I had spent my first weeks. My back muscles still ache from the strain of loading wet sheets into the wringer, while another girl turned the crank handle that squeezed the sheets through the rollers.

I've loathed the wringers since my first week in the

laundry when a girl became entangled in a sheet as a Consecrates turned the crank. The girl's hand was pulled into the wringer, her screams and the smear of blood on the white sheet are all I remembered when I woke from fainting. Later, on the way to dinner, I heard a whisper that the girl – Rosemary – had disobeyed a Consecrate and paid the penalty. The notion that someone would undertake such a hideous act left me horrified, and I began to understand that St Mary's was invested with many dangers.

The sewing room is in the same building as the laundry but is separated by a corridor of cupboards where the washing flakes and cleaning agents are stored. On the opposite side of the building is the ironing room, which, like the sewing room, is long and narrow with a row of windows that look out onto the gardens and dark forest beyond. Unlike the laundry, the greatest danger in the sewing room would appear to be boredom, and the occasional pinprick. We sit in three straight rows on hard wooden chairs, our baskets of sewing beside us, facing the large crucifix with its tormented figure of Jesus at the front of the room. Behind us is a table at which sits a Sister and her two Consecrates, while another three Consecrates, one in each line of penitents, sit halfway down the rows.

We are forbidden to speak, although the silence is occasionally broken by the murmur of a Consecrates' prayer. In this way the hours pass, sewing until our fingers cramp but with hearts lighter for the soft sunlight.

I was lulled into a false serenity in the sewing room, where even the Sisters seemed less threatening. The delusion was shattered by a cry of pain when Bernadette went into labour. At her first agonised wail, the true hideousness of the Sisterhood became evident for the room erupted into chaos and, as though a valve had been opened, the girl's pent-up anguish was abruptly released. They surrounded Bernadette, babbling and whining nervously as the girl, who was on her knees amid a spreading pool of fluid, begged Jesus to take away the pain.

My dismay was heightened by the sudden onslaught of Bernadette's labour. I know little of such events, although I was present when my mother went into her confinement with Lillian and James, but I was too young to understand what was happening. I have a vague recollection of Mother pacing the hallway of our house before disappearing into her bedroom with Dr Harrison, who came out hours later with a small, pink human that he said was somehow related to me. I remember also a conversation between my Aunt Cecilia and Mother over afternoon tea, about a month after my cousin Elise was born.

'It was the worst sixteen hours of my life,' Aunt Ceci said, around a mouthful of pumpkin scone.

My mother patted her hand and smiled. 'But what joy those sixteen hours have brought into our lives, my dear.'

Sixteen hours?

For Bernadette, it was over in less than sixteen minutes. Only later, in the dormitory, did I realise that she must have been in labour throughout the day. My heart filled with sadness at the thought of her sitting on our unforgiving wooden chairs, threading and stitching, as she endured the preparation of her body in silence.

However, at that moment, I thought only of helping the distraught penitent to the infirmary. I pushed through the circle of girls but I could see it was already too late. Bernadette was on her back, tearing at her thick stockings as she attempted to free herself from their constrictions. Her bonnet had slipped to the side, revealing her shaved head; the face beneath was contorted with agony and her breathing was ragged as her booted feet scraped against the floor.

Taking Bernadette's hand, I murmured words of encouragement, hoping to calm her and ease the baby's journey. On the other side of the withering girl, Charity was pulling away the last of the penitent's undergarments. She glanced at me and offered a faint smile, which disappeared as a keening rose from Bernadette. I looked down at the penitent, expecting her to be watching what she was doing. Instead, her eyes were locked onto something behind me. The keening began to articulate into a word and I realised she was saying 'no' over and over, like a plea.

I followed Bernadette's gaze to Sister Anslem, who stood amid the crowing girls, making no move to provide assistance. What I saw sent a chill through my soul and brought the Lord's Prayer to my lips. The nun was rigid with expectation, but it was her face that filled me with terror; strange silver-blue tendrils, like lightning, streaked her eyes and her mouth was stretched into an almost carnivorous leer.

Sweet Lord, is she human?

The thought vanished, unanswered, as Bernadette's baby came screaming into the world. Sister Anslem leapt forward, scooping up the babe, raw, pink and covered in blood. She tied off the umbilical cord with practiced ease and removed a large pair of scissors from the pocket of her habit. With a snip it was done, mother and child separated. The nun scuttled from the sewing room, the infant in her arms, leaving Bernadette wailing on the floor.

Sister Anslem's sudden departure had the same effect on the girls as a drenching with icy water. No one moved and the profound silence that filled the sewing room was broken only by Bernadette's wretched sobs as her body completed the afterbirth. Then Crispina, the Consecrate who had been sitting behind me through the day, ordered two of the girls to help Bernadette to the infirmary while the rest of us went back to work. As I took my seat, she pointed to me and motioned to Charity.

'You and you, clean up that mess.' I looked at the fluids Bernadette had expelled during the birth and was thankful lunch had passed some hours earlier.

Charity and I hurried from the room. Once in the hallway, I glanced at her and saw the paleness in her cheeks. She was clearly shaken by the birth, but it was difficult to offer her comfort as we are prohibited from speaking to each other. Such enforced silence is the Sisters' way of preventing friendships, which Sister Merce claims could lead to the creation of a 'wolf in the fold', who may jeopardise the virtue of her wayward charges.

However, as girls are wont to do, we find ways around such difficulties.

Walking side by side along the corridor to retrieve buckets, mops and cleaning cloths from the laundry, Charity and I murmured our thoughts through lips that barely moved. Of course, it's not a practice we undertake within the vicinity of the Sisters – not even those we consider safe, like Sister Sarah.

'What will happen to the baby?' Charity asked.

I had no truthful answer for her question, which was one I preferred not to consider since what I suspected was too horrid to contemplate, but the distress on Charity's face was hurtful to see and I wanted to ease her pain. 'There's an orphanage in the city,' I said vaguely, cursing the Sisters for forcing another sin onto my growing list.

'Do you believe that?' Charity asked.

Surprised, I risked a glance at her. The distress was still evident but her expression was also forthright.

'No,' I said.

'Me neither,' Charity replied, ending our conversation as we approached the laundry.

I lowered my head as we entered the steamy room. It would not do for the Sisters to see the relief and hope I was feeling. After months of doubt, I knew I was not imagining the menace at St Mary's. Charity knew the truth too. I shivered as I lifted a bucket into the sink and turned on the faucet. Horrifying as this realisation was, it was better to know the danger was real: we could not stand against a delusion of my mind but, as Father Michael insisted during the Mass, a good soul could stand against evil, and although the Sisters would insist otherwise, I knew my soul was untainted.

Order had been restored in the sewing room by the time we returned. The girls were sitting with heads bent to their work. At the Sisters' table, Crispina and Consecrate Winifred, sat on either side of Sister Merce, whose glacial gaze followed us as we hurried to the spot where Bernadette had given birth. My heart stuttered at the sight of the nun; I felt sure she suspected Charity and I. Kneeling, I kept my eyes averted and concentrated on scouring away the traces of miracle from that cold, unforgiving floor, knowing the Sister had reason to be suspicious. For in our few minutes alone, Charity and I had formed a bond; a Sisterhood of our own.

Page Twenty-Six

27th April 1906

It has been many days since I dared to write. The activities of the Sisters are becoming more feverish. Each day brings new humiliations, new cruelties and they are watching us closer than ever, waiting for a mistake that will justify their wrath.

Our workload has increased since Bernadette gave birth and we often labour in the laundries until late in the evening. We are forced to rise earlier to accommodate these demands. Yet working in the laundry is almost pleasant compared to Sister Merce's latest task, which she claims will redeem our corrupted souls.

The nun was waiting for us as we entered the dining hall for breakfast four mornings ago and, seeing the look on her face, my heart sank. Without preamble, she launched into her announcement. 'In one month, Monsignor Spalding will be visiting St Mary's. It has come to my attention that the driveway needs repairing before his Eminence arrives.'

The nun smiled as the magnitude of the task dawned on us. A narrow dirt track ran from the front gates to the convent. It had been worn into ruts over the years by foot and cart traffic but it was serviceable. I thought of the work ahead and of the condition of some of the girls – a few were only weeks away from delivering their babies – and groaned inside. Sister Merce watched closely, beaming.

Work on the driveway began that day and – Heaven forgive me – if this is what it takes to return to righteousness, I would gladly choose sin. There is, however, a silver lining to the nun's mad task. The dirt, heat, sweat and flies have made the Sisters and their Consecrates less vigilant, allowing Charity and I to share our stories. It is a risk, of course, but one I am more than willing to take if it allows our friendship to flourish.

Charity – her true name is Rachael – lived on the west side of the city with her parents, three brothers, and an older cousin, Jonas, who had been orphaned in the 1893 floods. Her family was part of the St Paul's congregation and she attended St Joseph's.

My heart sped up when she mentioned her parish and school, and I asked if she knew Patrick. She shook her head; she had attended the girls' college and interaction with boys was forbidden. I tried not to reveal my disappointment, however, Charity – she is rather sensitive, it seems – brushed my grime-covered hand with her own, all the while keeping her eyes on the ground so as not to draw unwanted attention.

When I had my emotions under control, I asked her how she came to be at St Mary's. I already knew why she was there – we were *all* there for the same reason; wicked girls that we are – and I was expecting to hear how she had fallen in love with a boy. What I didn't expect was the story of her defilement at the hands of Jonas, or the vile treatment she endured as her family first blamed then rejected her, turning their backs on the 'tramp' who had once been their adored daughter and sister.

Tears slipped down Charity's cheeks as she recounted the day the parish priest brought her to St Mary's almost six months to the day before I arrived. I squeezed her wrist briefly as I leaned over to pull out a clump of grass.

We did not speak for the rest of the day, knowing the risk of discovery increased the longer we engaged in conversation. We had learnt much about each other and it was enough to keep our minds busy while we worked.

Over the next three days, we shared our stories in snatches and then, when I felt sure I could trust her, I shared my secret of the attic. Two nights later, we crept from our beds and climbed into my haven above the sleeping girls. Charity tiptoed around the room, picking up a chalice or lifting a crucifix as the fancy took her. She smiled in the dimness as I lead her over to the bookcase. I slid Patrick's gift from amongst the Bibles and held it out.

I felt a tug in my chest as I thought of the sins I'd committed since I'd last seen Patrick, each one a weight on my heart. I could hear my mother voice, admonishing me in her no-nonsense way: *Upon such sins are built the tiers of Hell, Jennifer.*

I was tempted to confess to Charity as she took the diary but the opportunity slipped away with the opening of the first page. She turned from me and crossed to the window. Watching her read my most private thoughts, I knew this would be the test of our friendship. If she accepted what I had written as truth, I would have an ally; if not—

As this thought filled my mind, a stealthy sound came from the bottom of the stairs. Charity and I turned together, gazing at the dark entry to the attic, waiting and watching to see who or what was about to discover us. Seconds ticked by, each one an eon, as we

waited but the void leading down to the dormitory remained empty. We sighed in unison; it was time to
leave.

Charity closed the diary and handed it back so I
could hide it amongst the Bibles again. On our way
down the stairs – that first step into the dark stairwell
the most difficult of my life – she whispered, 'We must
not visit the attic together again. It is too dangerous.'

She was right. Then, just before we entered the
cupboard and pushed the door into place, she made a
suggestion, broached with a gentle shyness that further
endeared her to my heart. 'We could use the diary to
write to each other, that is, if it is not too precious to
you...'

I hugged her and whispered that it was a grand
idea.

And so, diary of mine, soon another's mark will
appear between your pages; the pure, sweet voice of
Charity.

Page Twenty-Eight

Dearest Grace,

I can't tell you what it means to finally have a friend in this hellish place. The last six months have been a nightmare and I've been filled with such despair. Even the Mass gives me no comfort, uplifting as Father Michael's sermons are, and I've thought, on my darkest days, that God has abandoned me, but then He sends you and my faith is restored.

I know I don't have a lot of time in the attic so I will skip over the mundane details of my time at St Mary's, which you know for yourself anyway: the work, the routine, the humiliation visited upon the 'Fallen'. Here is a question, Grace; just what've we fallen from? Didn't Jesus consort with sinner and saint alike, and forgive both when they strayed from God's path? What have we done that is so terrible that we are subjected to the Sisterhood?

Are such thoughts sinful? Maybe, but I'm convinced that our confinement here is a larger sin, one committed by our families, who have abandoned us, and our priests, who have turned away from us, believing they protect us from temptation. This might be true. I'm free of Jonas' lechery – although why I must suffer and not him, I don't understand – but when does this internment end? When is my redemption complete? I fear the answer is never.

Do you think I'm being melodramatic? Well, let me tell you about Cassandra and maybe you'll understand the future as I see it.

I'd seen Cassandra around St Mary's during my first three months: in the laundry, at mealtimes, and of course, at Mass. Like all the Consecrates, I gave her a wide berth even though, given her age, she was probably harmless as a babe in arms. *Probably*. Anyways, on this particular day, I was crossing the garden, making my way from the clotheslines to the laundry, when I heard a sob. It was a pitiful sound. I looked up and saw Cassandra staring at me.

I'd been at the convent long enough to recognise danger but, although I wanted to get on my way, the misery on the old woman's face stopped me. 'Are you alright?' I asked. I tensed for a berating, but she only gazed at me with her rheumy blues eyes. She murmured something I didn't catch and I knelt beside the stone bench she was sitting on, in the shade of the Poinciana, and asked again.

'They will not release me,' she whispered, tears slipping down her cheeks.

I hesitated, not wanting to upset her further, but I had to ask. 'Who won't release you?'

'I took the vow, it's true, but I was a strip of a girl then and I knew no better. I followed the others girls because they seemed so sure we would find our way back to the Almighty.' She grasped my fingers. '*But we did not know.*'

Her hand fell away as though her assertion had drained her. She was so frail. I wanted to wrap my arm around her shoulders and give her comfort but, I'm ashamed to admit, my sense of preservation was

119

stronger than my compassion and I remained kneeling.

'How long have you been here?' I asked. Confusion clouded her eyes and I thought quickly before asking the question again. 'How old were you when the Sisters took you in?'

'Eleven.'

I stared at her, horrified. If she was a day younger than eighty, I would eat humble pie. 'That means you have been here for—'

'Seventy three years,' she finished for me.

Can you imagine, Grace? Seventy three years in this Purgatory?

I pictured her in my mind as a girl; sweet and bubbly as a mountain stream, her whole life ahead of her and full of promises – love, marriage, and motherhood. None of it experienced. I held back my tears, for they wouldn't have been for her alone, and took her hand in mine, forgetting the differences between us. She smiled and squeezed my hand.

Then her mood changed. 'Run child,' she whispered. I frowned, unsure whether she meant right then, or from the life she saw before me.

The question became irrelevant as Sister Merce stepped around the Poinciana. 'Cassandra, we've been looking for you.'

The Consecrate shook off my hand and *snarled* at me to leave her alone. I shuffled backwards at the violence of her demand and toppled gracelessly to the ground.

Sister Merce turned her wintry gaze on me. 'Don't you have somewhere to be girl?'

I scrambled to my feet and hurried towards the laundry but, like Lot's wife, I couldn't help looking back. What I saw made me wish that I, too, had been turned to a pillar of salt. Sister Merce's hands were wrapped around the old Consecrate's throat. There was a loud snap and Cassandra's head lolled to the side as Sister Merce picked her up and carried her towards the convent. It was then I noticed the crows circling above the building, a black smear on the sky and I shivered, knowing whose soul they'd come to claim.

I've thought about Cassandra often in the last months; of her sad, wasted life and terrible death. I can't face that, Grace, so I've decided, since it's a mortal sin to take my own life, the only path left is escape. Wouldn't you agree?

Yours in friendship,

Charity

Page Thirty

Dear Charity,

Your story of Cassandra was so terrible that I could hardly contain my tears. The poor dear. We should take heart, however, knowing, at the very least, she has escaped the Sisterhood.

Escape.

How that word has plagued my mind and, after reading of Cassandra's dreadful passing, I know we must find a way to avoid the fate the Sisterhood would force upon us. With this in mind, let me tell you about Patrick – you remember I spoke of him in our first conversation? It was Patrick who gave me the diary that we share and Patrick who remains my hope of avoiding a future that seems, at the moment, inescapable. He is attempting to secure my release and I am sure, if I were to ask, he would speak on your behalf as well. If that fails, then I know Patrick will come up with some other rescue plan. Perhaps we could include you in our scheme?

Like you, sweet Charity, I do not want to live my life behind these walls, in drudgery and at the mercy of the Sisters. Yet, we can't deny the Sisters are a power to be reckoned with and we must not underestimate them, for to do so would surely result in our suffering, or worse.

Although I would dearly love to leave this place, I am aware that it may take some time to bring such a plan to fruition. We must work out every detail; we must watch and learn as much as we can about the Sisters, and we must wait until the timing is right and not act on impulse, no matter how difficult the circumstances. I do not know how long this will be, but patience must be our guiding principle. Of this, I am certain.

Perhaps we can take some comfort in the thought that, sooner or later, the Mother Superior will call the Sisters home to their Foundation. With any luck, the Sisters who replace them will be loving and sweet, like Sister Sarah, bless her soul. It is a faint prospect but, in this place, we must take hope where we can find it.

Yours,

Grace.

Page Thirty-One

Dear Grace,

I wish you could see my smile as I read your words, for the idea of escaping this place – whether through official means or by some extravagant plan – fills me with excitement. As you say, however, we must be patient and cautious as there are forces at work that we don't understand, although I do have an insight or two that I can share that might be useful to our planning.

First off, you mentioned a Foundation. There's something you must get clear – the Sisters of St Mary's are not ordinary nuns. In the time I've been here, I've never seen one of them leave the grounds, not even a step outside the gate, and there have been no official visitors from the Diocese either. Don't believe me? Ask yourself, did Monsignor Spalding arrive to inspect our new driveway? No, and he never will. I don't know how they do it but it would seem St Mary's is their Foundation and Sister Merce is the Mother Superior. There is no one coming to rescue us and no hope that the Sisters will abandon us either.

The second insight I have is this: the Sisters have been at their evil business for a very long time. I learned this from Consecrate Martha, who is the oldest inmate at St Mary's. Yes, I know everyone regards her as a doddering old fool but, if they took the time to listen to her mutterings, they would soon discover a frightening truth about Sister Merce and her Sisters.

You see (bear with me here), Martha talks to her dead brother. Amos is his name and a fine chap he is, if Martha is to be believed. I overheard her in the laundry one day, murmuring to Amos about the first time she had encountered 'that ancient daemon, Merce', when she was a child of eight. I don't know how old Consecrate Martha is but, with those wrinkles, I reckon she's got to be at least a hundred.

Now, if we put aside the 'talking to the dead' part that means Sister Merce was 'ancient' some ninety-five years ago. Have you looked at her, Grace? I know it's hard to tell with the cornette, but I wouldn't put her a day over thirty. How is that possible? I wish I knew for certain, but I only have theories, which you'll probably think outlandish. Still, I'll write them down and you can make up your own mind.

In my wildest flashes of imagination, I believe the Sisters have made a pact with the Dark One, who has granted them prolonged life for every ounce of misery they create, or for the souls they can steal. At other times, I think the Sisters are themselves demonic creatures that feed on the suffering of others, namely the girls they hold captive here at St Mary's.

Of course, these are only idle fancies but you have to admit there is something about the Sisters, something evil, that we must escape. So I'm with you on any plan you and Patrick might devise. However, we mustn't underestimate our enemy because to do so will most certainly prove to be fatal.

Your friend,

Charity.

Page Thirty-Two

My Dearest Charity,

Have you noticed an increase in the Sister's malice of late? It is as though they are reaching some crescendo in their zeal for punishing those who flout the rules.

I am thinking, as you will have guessed, of poor little Ava. Surely knocking over a statue doesn't warrant such a vile punishment as she is enduring? Yes, it was a statue of the Virgin, shattered beyond hope of repair. And yes, Ava was running in the corridor, late as she was for Confession, but to make the child stand in our Lady's place, arms outstretched, holding her pose, for hours – how long has she been there now? Five hours? There is no justice, no balance of penance and compassion in this ordeal, only cold retribution inflicted upon the most vulnerable amongst us.

Yet, as shocking as this punishment is, what causes me the deepest despair is the enjoyment the nuns take from Ava's predicament. They *stroll* past her – when do the Sisters ever stroll anywhere? – their eyes lit with enjoyment as the girl weeps.

If only someone from the outside could see them at times like this, certainly we would be set free. Yet, those beyond the walls never see what we see, so clever are the Sisters at hiding their true nature. Which is what? What is their true nature? Where did they come from? How can they treat us with such cruelty?

So many answerless questions, Charity, yet despite the Sisters' brutality, I must confess your theories regarding these matters seem somewhat implausible. I mean, demons and the Dark One? Are these not merely characters from stories meant to frighten young children? I do not mean to be dismissive, but I was not raised to believe in such superstitions.

Regardless of the truth, however, there is no doubt in my mind that escape is our only option. Indeed, it is vital, for we face an enemy who is powerful and cunning, and we risk being overwhelmed by their villainy if we are forced to remain here much longer. This is a fate I am not willing to accept.

Yet, I must at least contemplate the possibility, for what if Patrick fails? What if we find no means of escape? What if I must remain here for years? How would I survive? You have been at St Mary's longer than me, Charity. Have you seen any evidence of a weakness we may exploit? Is there a side to the Sisters I have yet to encounter? In your last letter, you wrote that the Sisters do not leave the grounds. Do you know why this is so? Does it mean that, if we can get past the walls and perhaps return to our families, we will be safe?

I do not mean to hound you. I should speak instead of pleasant things, of memories from my childhood, such as boating on the river with my family, or Sunday picnics in the park while the orchestra plays under the marquee. Or perhaps I should speak of the things that bring moments of joy here at St Mary's:

the warmth of the sun on our backs as we work, or the breeze that cools the sweat from our brows. Over such things, the Sisters have no control, for which we can rejoice, knowing that, perhaps, our keepers are not so all-powerful.

Yours,

Grace.

Page Thirty-Four

Dear Grace,

I've thought long and hard about your questions.

You asked if the Sisters have a weakness we could exploit. My answer is I don't believe so. It's true that I haven't seen the nuns leave the grounds in the time I've been here, but that doesn't mean they never have; after all, they had to come from somewhere before the convent was built. I think the secret of their power is here at St Mary's and that they want to stay close to it, but I'm not convinced that us being on the other side of the wall would offer much protection. Nor should you expect that your family would protect you from the Sisterhood.

Let me ask you, Grace, why do you think the Sisters get away with doing the terrible things they do to us in here? The answer is simple: no girl has ever left St Mary's in a state fit enough to tell the truth. To make matters worse, our families conspire to keep the practices of the Sisters secret, allowing them to continue their wickedness unchecked so that their own precious reputations remain untarnished. I've experienced this firsthand.

You remember Bernadette, of course. Well, I was there the day her parents threw her out of their carriage at the steps of the convent. I saw them drive away, stony-faced, as Bernadette scrambled after them, choking on their dust, begging to be taken home. Two days later, Bernadette absconded. The next day, her father brought her back to St Mary's. I was in the dormitory when he dragged her into the room by her hair and threw her across the nearest bed. Sister Assumpta and Sister Anslem stood behind him. They didn't intervene, not even when he took off his belt and whipped Bernadette when she tried to follow him out of the door.

No, Grace, put thoughts of your family out of your head. They bolster the Sister's strength, not weaken it. If we are to escape, we must accept that we are on our own in the world and that the only people we can rely on are each other. I know this must be disheartening and that our quest to be free of St Mary's may seem hopeless, but we can't let this stop us. Freedom must be ours.

Your Loving friend,

Rachael.

P.S. A thought occurred to me as I was leaving the attic. I don't have time to fully explain it, although I will try to be more detailed the next time I write. There is one strange thing I have noticed about the Sisters; they seem to have a peculiar distaste – almost an aversion – for the crows at St Mary's. It's a small thing, I know, which may amount to nothing, but it could also be worth investigating, just in case.

Page Forty

5th June 1909.

The most awful thing has occurred and I fear it is my fault because I introduced Charity to the diary and the attic. How clever I thought I was, how secretive and cunning, and now she has been caught by the new Sister.

Sister Dolorosa.

Just the thought of her sets my hand shaking. She is horror personified; the realisation of Charity's theory about the Sisters; demon in human guise. I don't know where she came from, nor when she arrived at the convent. We returned from the laundry for the midday meal and there she was, perched with the other Sisters at their table.

The nun wore the heavy black habit of the Sisterhood but it could not hide her sapling thinness. The black veil and cape, pulled tight around her face, intensified the shadows pooling in the hollows beneath her sharp blue eyes. Her mouth was a slash. She kept her back straight as though her frame was made of iron, and I knew instinctively she had a will to match.

This was no novice, but a new force with which to reckon. I sighed and she seemed to catch the sound. Her gaze latched onto mine and a humourless smile split her face as I took my seat.

If I'd listened to my intuition, I would have waited to see what new challenges Sister Dolorosa brought to the convent. However, the joy of sharing secrets was difficult to resist, and so when Charity climbed from her bed late in the evening and crept towards the attic, I smiled into my pillow, eager to read what she would write.

'Where are you off to, child?' Sister Dolorosa's voice was smooth as oil.

The dormitory woke. I heard Charity gasp, heard the beginnings of her stammered reply, then a sharp crack as the nun unleashed her fury. Squeaking springs drew my attention as Crispina left her bed. An instant later, the dormitory was filled with light and the full horror of the scene was illuminated. I screamed.

Charity was on her knees, her hands clutching Sister Dolorosa's arm at the wrist, her head tilted back, tears and blood mixing at the ugly split in her top lip as she stared imploringly at the nun who gripped her throat. In the Sister's other hand was a pair of black-bladed scissors. They plunged and I closed my eyes, unable to watch.

A sharp snip and my eyes snapped open. Charity was still kneeling but Sister Dolorosa had spun her around, grasped her between her knees, and was chopping away her hair.

With each snip she demanded to know where Charity was going and Charity – bless her – between her cries and struggles gave the same answer, 'To the bathroom Sister!' And when the hair cutting was over and the blows began again, her answer remained the same until finally, mercifully, she slipped into unconsciousness.

Sister Dolorosa delivered one last kick to Charity's prostrate form before turning to us. 'Let this one's mistake be a lesson to you all.' She stared hard at me and I lowered my gaze, wishing her gone so I could tend to my friend.

As the thud of Sister Dolorosa's boots faded down the hallway, I scrambled over and lifted Charity's head into my lap. Her eyelids fluttered and she whispered, 'We must get out.'

I looked to the door where the nun had gone, hatred filling my heart. Charity was right; to stay behind these corrupted walls would hasten my spiral into darkest despair. There had to be a way out. I touched Charity's bleeding face and knew risks would need to be taken, that sacrifices would need to be made, to secure the freedom we so desperately needed.

Page Fifty-Five

20th June 1909

I want to die.

I want this pain to end.

I want my heart to stop beating, but it goes on.

I want to stop breathing, but my chest refuses to be still.

I want my blood to turn to mud, but it surges through my body.

I want to sleep and never wake again, but sleep has vanished.

Yet this is good because – forgive me – for more than death, I want revenge.

Revenge on the Sisterhood; revenge on Sister Merce.

I knew something was wrong when I entered Contemplation two nights ago. Sister Merce was leaning against the lectern that held the Bible as we marched into the hall. She smirked at me and I was so shocked that I stopped walking. Hannah bumped into me and hissed as she gave me a shove to get me moving again. I slipped into my seat, feeling the nun's eyes on me as I crossed my ankles and pressed my hands together in prayer.

Charity took the seat across the aisle from mine; her face pale. I could see blue veins pulsing at her temple. The sight of the stubble sprouting from beneath her cap made my skin clammy. My friend had changed in the weeks since Sister Dolorosa had administered her beating; it was as though she was fading with the bruises that lined her jaw. My heart reached out to her. We had to find a way out of here. I thought of Patrick and dared to hope.

The rest of the girls took their seats and we sat with heads bowed, waiting. We knew any break in routine meant bad news was coming. The question was: bad news for whom? Time grew heavy and my shoulders ached with the pressure of keeping my head lowered. Was this what the condemned felt as they lay across the chopping block, waiting for the whistle of the guillotine as it fell, hungry and unforgiving, towards their exposed necks?

Sister Merce waited.

I flexed my shoulder muscles as I breathed out, easing my discomfort. Breathing in, I heard a new sound swelling beneath our oppressive silence – the girlish whispers of the Sisters as they filed into the room and took their seats.

I swallowed.

A sharp clap reverberated across the room as Sister Merce called us to attention and we straightened, hands in laps, eyes forward. Beyond the windows, a lone crow cawed as it wheeled across the darkening sky.

Sister Merce began with the greeting. 'The Lord's blessings be upon you,' but she did not wait for our usual response. Instead, she launched into a sermon that leached the warmth from my body with each word. 'Here at St Mary's we take pity upon, and offer sanctuary to, all manner of wayward creatures. None are turned from this house of our Lord and we welcome even those with the bleakest, most despoiled of souls, to our nurturing breast. This is a vocation, a calling if you will, laid down to my Sisters by the Lord and, although the challenge is great and the rewards small, we dedicate ourselves to His work, to the shepherding of His flock and the return of strays to His fold.'

There was a murmur of agreement from the other Sisters and the nun held up her hand to silence them. 'Within these walls lies the rare opportunity for young women who suffer the malaise of immorality, corruption, laziness, and selfishness, to find the righteous path, to repent of their sins and re-join our Father in his glorious kingdom. Who would not yearn for such an opportunity? What young woman would dare squander such a chance at redemption?'

I knew she was referring to me, even though her eyes swept over all of the girls. I shivered and wished for her to reach her conclusion, but from the twist of merriment at the corners of her mouth, I could tell she was enjoying herself far too much to hurry. And she wasn't the only one. Behind her, the other Sisters smirked and squirmed, expectant as children awaiting the beginning of a pantomime.

My feelings of dread increased.

At last, Sister Merce resumed. 'Alas, for some of you the prospect of returning to Grace is less appealing than the world of evil that lies beyond our gates. Yet we do not condemn you for this; even the wolf's serenade can seem attractive to a lamb waiting for slaughter. This we understand and thus, we acknowledge that our duty is to guide you back to the path *and* to shelter you from the tainted world beyond our boundaries. For your souls, it is the least we can do.'

With this pronouncement, she bowed her head in our direction, then turned and walked from the room. I stared after the nun in confusion and then risked a glance at Charity, who wore the same expression. My attention was drawn to the front of the room as a chair scraped.

Sister Dolorosa wasted no time. 'The body of a young man was found in the field beside the convent. A Patrick McManning, I believe. It seems he suffered a tragic accident in the night, which broke his neck. Presumably, he was trying to climb the wall to peer into the garden and has been punished by our all-seeing Lord.' Her thin fingers touched her forehead, sternum and each shoulder as she signed the cross. 'There will be strangers on the grounds over the next few days, officers from the city constabulary. They may want to speak with you regarding this misfortune. You will address these men briefly and only if they approach you, otherwise you will continue with your duties as usual.'

I don't know why Patrick's name didn't register with me at first; perhaps it was the matter-of-fact way the nun delivered the news. Or perhaps it was that I didn't want to hear, or that God in his mercy prevented the words from reaching me. Whatever it was, I didn't comprehend the dreadful news until Charity touched my hand.

Then the guillotine fell.

Page Fifty-Eight

23rd June 1909,

The Sisters released me from duties for two days; although they came in the night, whispering his name, drinking my grief. I let them sip heartily, to take as much as they wanted. What did I care? Patrick was dead and I wanted to die too – until I dreamt of that place.

I stood in a field of billowing black silk that was draped over everything: trees, rocks, rolling hills, streams and the majestic mountains behind me. The silk lifted, rising and falling as though a living, breathing entity. Above me, the sky was black and speckled with stars. A warm wind ruffled my hair, fluttering against my tear stained cheeks before slipping beneath my arms and giving me wings. Across this midnight landscape I flew until I saw a distant edifice, perched on the cliffs above a black lake. The stone walls glowed with an infusion of silver-blue light. As I drifted towards it, I felt coldness rising from the water's surface, and I shivered.

On the steps of the building was a familiar figure: Patrick. He shimmered, as though light was a protective cloak about his shoulders. The delight I felt at seeing him left me speechless but I needed no words as he drew me into his arms and kissed me. An eternity later, I heard his voice as he slipped a small round stone into my hand.

I glanced at the stone, which was icy against my palm. 'What is it for, Patrick?'

'Merce is not the first. You and three virtues must end her succession.' He curled my fingers around the stone. 'Use this amulet.'

'But, I don't understand,' I said, panic making my voice tremble. 'Patrick, please. What am I supposed to do?'

He laid his hand against my cheek. 'Grace is eternal. Faith is the guide. Hope draws the four. Charity never dies. Remember the Midnight Princes,' he murmured.

'I don't—'

'Hush, my love.' The black silk rustled around me, obscuring Patrick from my sight. Beyond the darkness, his voice came to me once more. 'I will love you forever.'

I woke at dusk on the third day to sunlight slipping through the dormitory windows, bathing the room in red hues of stillness. I struggled to re-establish my place in the world; the dream felt so real. My skin tingled with the lingering touch of silk and the cold from the stone throbbed through my hand. Was this what Joan of Arc felt when God sent her visions? If so, I could only hold her in greatest esteem, for the experience had left me drained.

What could Patrick have meant?

A chill shivered through my body and, as I drew my hands together beneath my chin to warm them, I realised the coldness emanated from within my clenched fingers. I held my hand out in the fading light. It seemed to belong to some other unfortunate girl. The cold seeped deeper into my skin. I forced my fingers open. On my palm lay the amulet, its surface dissected

139

by two intersecting lines dividing it into quadrants.

A confusion of thoughts burst through my mind as the dark stone gleamed. What did it mean? How could it be here? What was I to do with it? Fear welled in my chest and I gripped the stone in my fist.

From the stairs beyond the dormitory came the creak of footsteps. The girls were returning from Confession. I sat up and glanced around the room, my fear intensifying as I looked for somewhere to hide the amulet. Finally, I deposited it inside my bodice, knowing the hiding place was only temporary.

'Ah Grace, I see you've decided to rejoin us,' Sister Sarah said, as she lead the girls into the dormitory, 'and just in time to assist in the preparations for dinner. Sister Merce will be pleased. Wash up with the others and make your way to the kitchen.'

'Yes Sister.'

My reply was automatic as I was more concerned with capturing Charity's eye. She was standing behind Crispina, waiting her turn to use the washroom and, although I moved towards her, she kept her gaze on the floorboards. I joined the end of the line and watched as she washed her hands and face, then re-entered the dormitory. Her pale skin was more translucent than when I had seen her at dinner two nights earlier. I swallowed the sour taste of fear and wondered at her decline. As she passed me, I inched out of line, hoping to touch her but she did not acknowledge my presence.

Something has happened to Charity while I was mourning Patrick. There is a distance between us that I don't understand. One thing is certain, however, the Sisters will be at the heart of the divide.

Page Sixty-Two

1st July 1909.

Damn this cursed place. I pray to God for this to end but, instead, the situation grows more desperate by the day. Has He forsaken us, the fallen girls of St Mary's?

Charity weeps and not even sleep brings her relief. She is a shadow of herself since the beating at the hands of Sister Dolorosa. How evil that one is; how she gloats whenever she encounters Charity and the poor girl seems not to have the fortitude to withstand the torment much longer.

We must leave this place but whenever I try to discuss some means of escape with Charity, she looks at me with horror. There is something in her eyes that is like a scream. What is it that I am missing?

To occupy my mind, I have taken to thinking on my dream and its significance. It is not lost on me that Grace and Charity – the very names given to us by the Sisterhood – were part of Patrick's message, but what of Hope and Faith? There are no penitents at St Mary's with these names. Was he speaking, then, of the Christian virtues? If so, how do these four elements fit together? If I turn to the Scriptures, they would tell me that these are the virtues needed to live a good life. However, it seems to me that there is more to Patrick's message; a key to ending the terror stalking our lives. I wonder, too, about the amulet. What does it mean? What does it do? Questions, question, questions, and yet the answers remain elusive and my frustration increases by the hour as I watch the Sisters grow bolder and more outrageous in their cruelty.

My anxiety to hear Charity's views on the amulet did not lessen during the days following its strange appearance. I continued to try and gain her attention but she steadfastly refused to be drawn into communication with me. Instead, she hunched her shoulders and turned away. Finally, I gave up, fearing the Sisters would catch my attention seeking. Still, I knew I could not keep the knowledge of the amulet secret much longer; after all, it involved Charity as much as myself.

I waited until the dormitory was plunged into darkness last night before I took the amulet from its hiding place inside my bodice. I hadn't dared let it out of my sight, suspecting its importance, if not its purpose. I ran my finger over the intersecting lines and let my mind drift, seeking answers. Later, being no closer to the secret of the thing, I crept from my bed and tiptoed over to Charity.

She was awake. Her breathing was punctuated with soft hiccups and I knew she'd been weeping again. My heart clamped with sadness as I placed a soothing hand on her shoulder, wishing I could remove her grief and fear.

Although I knew the danger was great, I whispered for her to follow me to the attic. I felt her body grow rigid. The idea that she would refuse occurred to me but I pushed it away; we were friends. Still, she lay there so long I was about to return to my bed, then I heard her sigh. She pushed aside the covers and I hurried towards the attic, knowing she'd follow.

Charity crossed the floor beams to the window where I was standing, taking quick, light steps that revealed her annoyance. 'This is sheer stupidity,' she whispered, drawing away from me even before she finished speaking. Rather than try to persuade her to stay, I held out the amulet.

The stone was dull in the meagre light. Charity stared at it blankly. The look on her face was easy to read: *You put me in danger for that?* She was taking another step away when the amulet flared into life, surprising us both. Charity gasped and I gazed at the object resting on my palm, fascinated. In the centre of the stone, where the two lines intersected, light particles began to gather, forming a twisting column like a whirlwind. The pillar twirled faster and when it was a perfect cone, it burrowed into the amulet, spreading out until the quadrants were suffused with light.

The amulet gleamed silver-blue but remained cold against my skin until Charity placed a hesitant finger on the stone. A low hum vibrated across my palm to the tips of my fingers, up through my wrist and into my body. I breathed out, causing the air around us to shimmer like a heatwave. The sensation was surprising and I laughed with delight.

Charity snatched her finger away and pushed her hand against my mouth to silence me, her eyes darting to the stairwell. When she felt sure we had not been overheard, she looked at the amulet again, which had returned to its cold dark state.

Then the questions came: 'What is that? Where did it come from? What just happened? What does it mean?'

I answered her as best as I could, telling her of the dream – but not of Patrick's rhyme; somehow I could not bring myself to reveal it to her – and of how I came to have the amulet. She listened intently, not interrupting until I finished.

'Will it help us escape the Sisterhood?' she asked.

At her words the amulet vibrated briefly and I closed my hand around it. During the long months since coming to St Mary's, I had dreamed of escape, thinking of ways impractical and fanciful of achieving the freedom my heart so desired. Was it any less far-fetched to believe that a rock, which had materialised out of my dream, could be the key to liberation? Did I want to build our hopes on such a fancy?

Charity touched my arm. 'I don't know,' I replied, closing my fingers around the amulet. 'I need more time to work out its purpose, but maybe.' I offered her a faint smile and she nodded.

'We should go back to the dormitory,' she said and hurried away.

At the top of the stairwell, Charity stopped. She leaned close and whispered, 'We need to be more careful. The Sisters are watching.' I nodded, but she was already halfway down the stairs, leaving me to return to the dormitory alone.

True to her word, Charity adopted an even more cautious approach when I was near, refusing even to look at me when we passed in the corridors. Although I tried to be understanding, the seeds of doubt grew within me whenever I encountered her diverted gaze. *Was she hiding something?* I wondered; a question that became a sickening certainty when I saw Charity being shepherded into Sister Merce's office by Sister Assumpta. Dread washed over me as the diary and amulet came to my mind. *What do the Sisters want with her?* As the door closed behind her, I decided we should meet again, sooner rather than later.

I waited on the old pew and watched Charity from the shadows as she crept up the stairs, reading the exhaustion in her face, knowing it was mirrored in the dark smudges beneath my eyes. Sleep had become a precious gift since the amulet came into my possession and, although the Sisters were as dangerous as ever, the chaotic state of my mind was not entirely their fault. It was the dreams.

Every night they came to me, filled with visions of Patrick, of a thousand birds taking flight, of a silver-blue light, of the amulet full of fire, of Sister Merce's gloating face, and of Charity laying lifeless at the edge of a black lake. The images haunted me by night while by day, my restless mind circled them, searching for their meaning.

Charity slumped onto the pew beside me and rested her head against my shoulder, her fatigue hanging around her like a heavy woollen shawl. She was silent but suddenly my head was full of visions; dead crows, a building reduced to a pile of rubble, the smouldering remains of a pile of bones and a faceless girl I knew to be Charity on the edge of the same black lake from my dreams.

I shuddered. *To achieve victory, sacrifices must be made.* The thought tumbled across my mind. *Who had said that?* I wondered. *Napoleon, perhaps?*

As I looked towards the window, thinking about my dreams and the idea of sacrifice, Charity slipped her hand into mine. It was cold and thin but I held it tight as the words to Patrick's rhyme fell like snow inside my head.

Grace is eternal.
Faith is the guide.
Hope draws the four.
Charity never dies.
Remember the Midnight Princes.

'You know what to do now, don't you?' Charity asked.

I nodded because I didn't trust my voice. The fact was I did know what to do, but to follow that course lead to an unthinkable conclusion: Charity at the edge of the black lake. The thought filled me with a dread larger than anything I felt for the Sisters.

'Are you sure it will work?'

Although I wanted to shout a denial, I didn't speak because I knew we had no choice in the matter for, in my last dream, Patrick gave warning that the Sisters knew something was afoot.

'How do they know?' I asked him.

'Ask Charity, she knows all,' he replied as the dream began to fade.

I looked at Charity in the light spilling through the attic window, casting half her body in shadow. Her head had drooped and her chin was resting against the hollow of her chest. She seemed so delicate that I feared to breathe in case the sound caused her to shatter. What had brought her so low? What had she been doing in Sister Merce's office?

Perhaps I should've followed Patrick's advice and asked her these things, but her fragile state convinced me that the time for questions had passed. We had to act or be lost forever. The decision made, I felt a surge of determination, yet I couldn't help wondering why my heart was beating like the wings of a trapped bird.

Page Sixty-Eight

7th July 1909,

God save me. I was wrong. The price! The price was too high. Oh sweet Charity, what have I done? How could I have thought so poorly of you? The blood! Oh God, the blood pouring from your torn throat, and that hideous gagging. I shudder to remember yet I cannot erase it from my mind.

Forgive me, Charity, but who could have known the Sisters' power? Why didn't Patrick give warning? And now they hunt for me. I hear them outside as they follow my footprints over the frosted grass, to the laundry door, which I've barred as best I can, but it won't be long before they find me, before they break in and then—

I must finish this last entry before hiding the diary in the hope that it will find its way into the hands of one who knows the truth. Oh, what did I know? What was it that was hidden in the shadows but the other two? Faith and Hope; virtues stripped from our hearts long before this confrontation. And the crows, the midnight princes – those foes – who would have guessed? But I must gather my thoughts and tell of this morning; of Charity's final dawn.

We chose the time when we believed their power

was on the wane. I could sense Charity's fear but her face was set with resolve as we approached Sister Merce's office. In my hand, the amulet was as cold as a clod of dirt, but still, I didn't falter. Oh, foolish girls that we were, what did we hope to achieve, confronting our enemy with such little preparation?

What if we'd run when the door to Sister Merce's office swung open? Would we have escaped this fate? Possibly not, and it was not an option, for Charity didn't hesitate, even though she knew what was in my mind; the distrust that had festered in me during our last weeks together. Instead, she slipped her hand into mine and, as our palms met, the amulet fired, sending a shaft of light into the room.

Shapes moved inside, darting out of the beam that cut through the dimness. A squeal, like a pig caught by the hoof, reverberated around the room. The sound was cut off by the slap of flesh against flesh and an angry hiss, demanding silence. We crossed the threshold, hands throbbing with light and heat, hearts filled with courage – but missing the most important virtues of all.

She was sitting behind the solid desk, her bone-white face within the black circle of her habit floating in the darkness. The blood seemed to freeze in my veins but Charity urged me forward. Oh, what fortitude she had in those moments, my brave, brave girl. Not even when Sister Dolorosa came flying at us from the shadows did she flinch. Instead, she pulled my arm upwards, drawing on some secret knowledge of her own, and turned the light upon the howling wretch.

The shaft hit her at the hollow of her throat and wrapped around her, squeezing. The nun dropped to her knees as though praying, a strangled sound issuing from between her lips, which frothed with pink-tainted saliva. That's when I heard them; the same moment the battle was lost. The crows beat their wings against the window in a fury, screaming for entry. I heard a crack and then the panes imploded. They flew at us, engulfing Sister Dolorosa.

Charity's hand released mine, the light from the amulet dying as we lost contact. Sister Merce appeared out of the cloud of wings. She reached for Charity, who turned to me and yelled, 'Run!' as the nun gripped her throat, fingers sinking into Charity's flesh as she pulled.

Father in Heaven, forgive me, but I did as Charity said. I ran, looking back only once, and what I saw tested my sanity, for the nuns were no longer human. No, and they crowded around Charity as her eyes rolled and that sound, that sound—

I ran into the back garden, past the clotheslines, to the last place I had seen Patrick. My only thought was to hide the amulet and then find refuge, somewhere I could take a moment to think: the attic. I looked above the dormitory as I raced across the grass and saw a cloud of darting crows. Cursing them, I slipped inside and darted up the stairs, through the empty dormitory, to the linen closet. The dimness of the attic was a relief and I felt a sense of peace as I took my diary from its hiding place and held it close to my heart. I seemed to hear Charity's sweet voice in my head. Then her tone changed, became urgent, insistent. 'Get out, get out, get out!'

I ran again; through the dormitory, down the stair and into the fresh morning air, just as a howl of rage came crashing through the door behind me. I lifted my skirts and sprinted for the nearest building that might offer some protection; the laundry. If I could hold them off, perhaps Father Michael would come along after morning prayers and I could signal for him. The hope was small, but it was all I had.

Still, it seems to be a hope in vain; just as our foolish attempt to escape the Sisterhood was in vain. Why didn't I see it before? Is it only under extreme circumstances that full understanding comes to us? How is that fair? How are we to fight the good fight if we can't understand all of the nuances until after the battle is lost? Yet, perhaps the answer was there in Patrick's rhyme – Faith, Hope, Grace and Charity. Without the four virtues, there can be no victory, no relief from this evil.

Oh Lord, I hear the crows on the roof of the laundry; and the Sisters—

The Sisters are inside.

Part Three

The Book of Four Virtues

Joie de Vivre

In the Garden of harmony,
Down the boulevard of Creation's chaos,
A melody unravelling, one song of adulation,
The symphony on splendid wings,
Unfetters the perpetual moment.

In the abode of wisdom,
The dweller resides serene,
In the dale verdant,
Where angels dance,
And the four winds entwine,
Carrying the eternal present,
To the feast of unity,

In the meadow resplendent manifests,
the power of Imagination,
Abundant,
Of effervescent Grace.
Oh Arcadia! Beautiful Arcadia,
Amid your vibrant bounty,
Lies the salvation of
Now.

Chapter One

Mama says I was born "knowing". She says my eyes shone with an ancient wisdom as I came into the world. She says the nurses saw it too, and that they looked at me with awe as they cleaned me up and wrapped me in white cloth. Of course, some might say my mama was affected by post-birth bias, or was high on pethidine, but they'd be wrong.

I'm not trying to big note myself here. The way I understand it, all babies are born with this knowledge, but most people forget as they grow older and become more reliant on the outside world for their sense of purpose. They shut down their innate senses and entomb their gifts as they become adults. I'm not passing judgement; it just the way it is— for most people.

For me, the knowledge I was born with is encoded in my mind. Sometimes I can draw on it consciously; other times it sneaks up and pounces, digging in its claws until I bleed. It hurts when that happens but I learnt early not to resist. Surrender is the easiest choice.

If I think about how I came to be at St Mary's, if I follow the chain of events, it's clear I've been in training all of my life to use this knowledge in the confrontation that's coming. That training began the day I meet Leon.

Mama had taken me to the park. I was two, or there abouts, and excited by the bright colours and strangely shaped objects in the sandpit. Mama sat on the bench seat beside a harassed young mum, who was swamped by children. One of them, a boy a few years older than me and wild as a cyclone, fell off the swing and came up screaming. The two mums rushed to him and that was when Leon swooped.

He clamped a hand over my mouth and lifted me into his arms. The stink of tobacco and something else – sour milk perhaps – curled from his thick fingers. I squirmed in his grip, reaching back towards my mama with my hands. A soft breeze lifted the strands of my hair, brushing them against Leon's rough cheek. He grunted and squeezed me harder.

Fear, like a cloud of flies, buzzed through my body. Not because I knew what Leon wanted but because the soothing babble of voices that lived in my head suddenly roared; a Niagara Falls of warning gushing through my mind. I whimpered and Leon glanced at me.

'Hush baby,' he muttered.

A crow answered him. As its cry faded, the clamour in my head subsided, leaving one musical voice. She sang to me, a song of escape, and I knew how to get away. I opened my mouth and sank my teeth into Leon's fingers. Leon yelped and dropped me. For a moment, I could do nothing except suck air into my lungs. Then I howled.

I watched Leon lope across the park, my tears drying even as Mama scooped me into her arms, cradling me to her chest as she cooed my name, but I wasn't listening to her.

Good girl. Brave girl. Sweet girl, sang a voice in my mind that belonged to someone called Grace.

There have been others like Leon, though none who'd come as close to doing me harm. Until now. The nun who calls herself Merce – that's not her real name, by the way. Once she was called Dinah and before that, Clementina, but her first name was Caritas, or so Grace told me. Anyway, when Merce and her Sisters are near they set off the voices in my head and I have to suppress the urge to groan. I didn't tell Faith about that – no need to freak the girl out. She's tough, and she's seen her share of shit in here, but explaining that I could hear the psychic manifestation of the Sister's evil might test the boundaries of our friendship, and I can't risk her flipping out. I need Faith to get through what's coming.

My voices have gotten me out of some tricky situations over the years. In eighth grade, for instance, they came to the rescue when my teacher, Mr Abernathy, asked me to name the levels of Parliament. Ordinarily, this would've been a cinch, but I'd been daydreaming about Jarred Morrissey who sat three seats down from me. I stared at Mr Abernathy as though he'd asked me to name the chemical composition of a black hole. Then, just as every kid in the class – including Jarred Morrissey – turned my way, my voices whispered the correct answer, saving me from permanent loser status.

More importantly, my voices help me out on the home front as I try to navigate the minefield that is life with Mama, who's a woman with two basic states of existence: neurotic and totally irrational. Each has pitfalls and benefits. When she's neurotic, she pretty much ignores me. At the other end of the scale, when she's having a full-on irrational episode, she might lock herself in her bedroom (acceptable), or decide it's time for some one-on-one mother-daughter time (which translates into *Confessions of a Forty-Four Year Old Single Mother*. God, kill me now). Either way, my voices sense her temperament and I adjust my levels of visibility accordingly.

The only time my voices failed me was with Caleb. Somehow, he slipped by their protective vigil and stole my heart away before they could raise a murmur, but that was as it should be because Caleb had lessons to teach me about love and forgiveness. These were the last lessons I needed to learn before I faced the Sisterhood.

Most people would say we were too young to understand love. They'd say it's only with experience, with time, that an understanding of another person grows into something meaningful and complete. They'd say what Caleb and I had was 'puppy love'. They'd say it would never last because we didn't have the maturity to stand the test of time.

Bullshit.

I say we're born to love; it's our purpose. And it doesn't matter when love comes, or in what form. Hell, I fell in love with my Grandma Violet when I was six; used to follow her around and listen to her stories while she collected vegies from her patch out in the backyard. Was I too young to understand and feel love then? No, and that's because, when you meet someone who lights up your world, it's love and it's right. But what Caleb and I had wasn't right in the eyes of the 'adult' world, as my mama proved.

When she saw Caleb and I together in my bedroom that last morning; our skin touching, our mouths pressed together, our bodies entwined, she went a little crazy and, for a moment, I didn't recognise her. The face I'd known my whole life melted away and underneath was a gibbering, insane creature. Then, as though sensing exposure, the mask dropped back into place and she was Mama again.

Before she leapt at Caleb and chased him out of the house, I looked at him, wondering if he'd seen her real face too. How do I describe him, standing in the shafts of light piercing my window? Like my mother, Caleb seemed to be many people caught in the one body: he was a sorrowful boy caught doing something naughty, who didn't know how to make it right; he was a swaggering I-don't-give-a-fuck teenager with a finger shoved in the air; he was a man struggling with his responsibility; and a lover, looking at me with tenderness in his sad eyes.

Stronger than all of these, though, was the addict: switched off, shutdown, lights-on-but-nobody-home, blank. It was this Caleb who watched my mama impassively as she yelled insults into his face.

My heart broke to see this shadow-Caleb but I began to understand why he used. How many times had he been lashed by the world; my mother being the latest whipping master? Why couldn't she see what she was doing? Why couldn't she shut up and look at him for one second? Why couldn't she see what her anger was doing to him? To me? To all of us?

I hated her then, as she hounded Caleb down the stairs, spewing her fury. She slammed the door after him and my hatred grew. I sat on my bed as she pounded up the stairs again, cursing him as the foulest cretin to ever walk the planet, and I vowed to hate her forever.

Yield and overcome, Grace whispered.

No, I replied.

'There's only one place for girls like you,' Mama shouted as she came into my room.

'For girls like me? And just what sort of girl am I, Mother?'

Yield and overcome. The other voices joined with Grace, insistent as breathing.

I can't.

I glared at my mama, seeing her struggle to hold back the words she wanted to use to describe me, her mouth trembling with the effort. Maybe it was her restraint that softened my resolve. More likely, it was the pressure of the voices, chanting their demand:

Yield and overcome.
Yield and overcome.
Yield and overcome.

Mama did her Zen thing: deep breathe in, exhale slowly, and said, 'I can't do this anymore. The Sisters will take care of you.'

'What sisters?' I asked, sensing something coming like thunder after a lightning strike.

'You'll see,' she said, marching from my room.

Yield and overcome.

'Whatever,' I replied, crawling under my doona. I felt like a battle-weary soldier, who'd spent the day losing ground. Sleep was the only place where I could win a reprieve, but I knew it would be hours before I could surrender completely.

And when I did—

Caleb held my hand and led me through the cemetery. Around us was the fragrance of growing things: grass, flowers, shrubs. I could hear the rustle of insects and something larger in the trees. I drew a breath and spluttered as the sharp reek of decay filled my lungs. The growing things withered, died, and blew away down a long avenue lined with tombs.

We came to a mausoleum. The grey marble door was cracked down the centre. Light flickered through the gap. Caleb squeezed my fingers and I found myself inside the crypt, alone, breathing stale air. A single candle stub burned against the far wall, upon which was inscribed:

To Begin
One must end.
Forgiveness is the key.

Caleb appeared by my side and I looked at him, a question forming on my lips. He smiled and a ball of twisted crucifixes fell from his mouth. I woke up with my hands pressed to my face, stifling my scream.

For three nights Caleb came and walked me through the graveyard until, finally, on the fourth morning, I went down to the kitchen and made Mama breakfast: coffee, juice, toast and a bowl of fruit. I took the breakfast to her room and knocked before I went in. She was already awake, lying in the gloom. I put the tray on her bedside table and waited.

She looked from me to it and back again, then she sat up and fluffed her pillows. 'This changes nothing,' she said.

'Yes Mama,' I replied, knowing it changed everything.

Surrender.

That night, Caleb led me through a long, vaulted room filled with warm, soft colours. I looked at the ceiling in wonder and saw the roof was made of stained glass: angels, cherubs and nymphs danced there; birds swooped through ancient gardens and animals frolicked beside a lake the colour of ink. I wanted to stop but Caleb urged me forward.

'Another time, Dao-girl,' he said.

We walked on, until we came to a pair of gates. They rose before us, twisting black iron stretching into the heavens. On the other side: darkness.

Caleb touched the gates and they swung open.

'I don't want to,' I whispered, as he released my hands.

'She needs you,' he replied, nodding towards a girl coming out of the gloom.

I drew a sharp breath, recognising her. She smiled and I felt my mouth curve in response but still I resisted. There was something moving in the darkness above her, and as she reached the gate and held out her hand to me, the air was filled with screaming crows. I covered my ears and closed my eyes, bracing for the impact of their descent, but there was only silence.

In my own darkness, I heard Grace's voice. 'Find Faith and come to me.'

So I found Faith, but now I'm losing her. I can see it in her eyes, in the way she searches for me. I want to reassure her but how can I explain? This is how it is before the answers come.

I know what she's thinking, and I don't mean figuratively. I really do know. I'm not saying I can read her mind or any weird shit like that; I sort of interpret the secret language of her body. Not that she's very good at hiding her feelings, which are as obvious as a neon-lit billboard. She's wound up 'cause she wants me to explain how it's possible for Merce and her cronies to be the same nuns that tormented the 'fallen' women of Grace's time.

I don't have a straight answer for her. 'It's a paradox you need to accept, Faith.'

'Oh right,' she says, waving the diary through the air like she might throw it across the room. She paces the attic. 'I should accept that Sister Merce is over a hundred years old? And while I'm doing this *accepting*, maybe I should just accept all the bizarre coincidences between what's in this stupid diary and the stuff we deal with at St Mary's?'

'There *are* no coincidences; everything is linked,' I reply, moving to the window. Something's out there, odd shapes moving in the moonlight. 'For example, if you don't stop making all that noise, the Sisters will hear you and then we'll be fucked.'

The pacing ceases. 'I know you're right,' Faith says as she leans against the wall beside me. 'Deep inside, I know that, by some strange design, the Sisters have managed to cheat death, but what good does that do us?' Her voice is taut. 'What are we supposed to do about the Sisterhood if the nuns are all powerful, super-evil, time-defying demons, or whatever? It was hard enough surviving them when they were just regular psychos. But now what? Are we expected to defeat them and restore goodness to the world? And just how are we supposed to do that, huh? Bore them to death by reciting the *Our Father* ten thousand times? Strangle them with their Rosary beads?' She snorts, humourlessly. 'At least that's a physical possibility; imagine garrotting Sister Merce.' She shakes her head. 'What a great, big, fat, joke on every poor girl who's ever been locked up in here. Ha ha, very funny.'

I stay quiet during Faith's rant, not because I'm ignoring her but because there are some things I don't want to waste my breath explaining. The Sisterhood is here; we're here; we have to defeat them. Simple. How we do that is something I'm working on – if Faith would shut up and let me. I press my hand to the window; out in the garden, the crows are doing something unusual.

Every now and then one ruffles its feathers and flutters from its perch in the pine trees down to the driveway, where it takes a piece of gravel in its beak. After a moment, the bird lifts off, circling over the church, before landing in the Poinciana, where it deposits the gravel in the fork of the tree.

What the hell?

'Hello?' Faith snaps her fingers in front of my face.

'Are you listening to me?'

'No.'

'What?'

Honesty's a bitch. 'Nothing,' I say, pointing to the tree. 'Have you ever seen crows do that before?'

Faith watches the birds. 'That's strange.'

'Yeah, and it means something.'

'Sure. Like everything else around here, the crows are bloody weird.'

I roll my eyes – *so cynical* – and continue watching the crows gather their stones and hide their treasure.

Hide their treasure?

A light flickers inside my head and I grab Faith's arm, pulling her through the attic. 'Come on, we need to get some sleep.'

'What? Why?'

'Because tomorrow we're going on a treasure hunt.'

'What are you talking about?'

'The amulet.'

'The amulet?' Faith asks, trying to stop but I keep her moving.

'Ah-huh, it's the key.'

'The key to what?'

'To everything.'

'What does *that* mean?'

'Not sure. Guess I'll know when we find the amulet.'

'But we know where it is. Grace wrote in the diary that she hid it in the wall.'

'She did, but it isn't there anymore.'

We stop at the entrance to the linen cupboard. 'How could you know that?' Faith asks.

'Grace told me.'

'What?'

I shake my head. 'Later.'

But she's not moving until she has an answer.

'Grace from the diary?' I nod, glancing towards the doorway. Faith smiles, her mouth crooked with uncertainty.

'Look, you're gonna have to trust me on this, okay?' I say, giving her arm a reassuring squeeze. The smile disappears. I'm freaking her out after all, but she'll get used to it, especially once we find the amulet, because – if Grace's right – that's when things will really get crazy.

Chapter Two

There are two things I've always been good at; attracting the attention of guys and solving riddles. The guy thing's easy. When I was younger, I was one of the boys. I could out fight, out spit and out play any guy at any game. Of course, they didn't know I had a little help on the 'inside' and I was careful never to let on. Guys are so full of themselves sometimes and not many like being beaten by a girl – not at their own games – so I never got too cocky (excuse the pun), never bragged about winning and soon I was just another mate who kicked arse at whatever we were doing. Of course, once puberty and curves set in, the guys didn't want to play those games with me anymore; but I soon learnt how to win at that game too.

The riddle thing is harder, although like with guys, some are easy to work out:

> *When one does not know what it is, then it is something;*
> *but when one knows what it is, then it is nothing.*

Mama told me that one over a breakfast of raw egg and cranberry juice (crazy fad diet number nine). It'd taken her a day to work it out and once she got it, she thought it was the cleverest thing she'd ever heard.

I blame the juice.

There are other riddles that hold their secret long

enough to bring me to the point of frustration but, in the end, I always get them. One of my favourite is by this guy called Herbert. He posed the question: How many angels can dance on the head of a pin, and then offered a riddle as the answer:

How wondrous too is the truth received
For him who'd defy verity
As hope the sick soothes even sates
So benign the uncertain's made.

The strange thing about the riddles is, when I came up against one that I have to struggle to solve, the voices in my head are always silent. Not gone, but sitting back as if they know I need to work out some stuff for myself. The riddle of the amulet is a case in point: the voices held their peace, even though Grace must've known the object's purpose.

Finding the amulet wasn't hard, though it took a few days. Grace told me she'd moved it before the old wall surrounding the school was demolished and replaced by the perimeter fence that keeps us concealed from the world, but she wasn't specific about its hiding place. I guess she wanted me to work for that answer too.

Except it wasn't me who figured it out. It was Faith.

We were working in the garden, weeding dandelions from the lawn, when it happened. I was busy trawling around in my head, obsessing over the riddle of the amulet when I realised Faith wasn't beside me; she was crouched on her haunches, staring over at the Poinciana.

I ripped out a weed and sent her a death stare, which she ignored. 'I've been thinking about the crows from the other night,' she said. 'And about Cassandra.'

I tossed a clod over my shoulder, sprinkling her with dirt. 'Who?'

She brushed the earth away absently. 'You know, the old Consecrate from Charity's letter,' she said, standing and walking towards the tree.

'Hello? Where are you going?' I called after her, glancing at the dormitory. Clearly, she'd forgotten our all-knowing, all-seeing captors. Faith walked around the Poinciana, her fingers trailing over the bark. That's when it hit me, like a great invisible hand smacking me up the side of the head. I crossed the lawn, joining Faith as she climbed onto the stone seat.

Her hand dipped into the fork of the tree, first up to her wrist and then, as she rose onto her toes, up to her elbow. She looked into the tangle of branches above, not seeing with her eyes, but with her mind as her fingers searched. A smile lit her face as she withdrew a small package, wrapped in yellowing cloth. Stepping down, she put the package in my hand and we stared at it for a moment, absorbing its reality.

Faith nudged me. 'Go on.'

My fingers shook as I folded back the stiff cloth. The amulet was just as Grace described: a black, round, palm-sized stone intersected by two deeply etched lines. It was snow cold to touch.

'It's real,' Faith murmured.

I could only nod. Holding the amulet confirmed everything, which meant there was no escaping what I'd been called to do. I closed my hand around the stone and looked at Faith. 'How did you know where to find the amulet?'

'I didn't know exactly. I sort of connected the dots: the crows, Cassandra, the Poinciana.'

Above us, a crow cawed as though in warning. I gave Faith another appraising glance before taking a quick look around the tree, making sure we hadn't been spotted by the Sisters. The grounds were empty. I slipped the amulet into my pocket and grabbed Faith's hand, leading her back to the lawn; we still had the weeding to finish.

As we bent to the task, I could feel the amulet against my leg. Excitement flashed through me. *Focus, girl*, I reminded myself, *soon the real work begins*.

We weeded silently until Faith stood up to stretch. 'I know the amulet is important and all that,' she said.

'Not just important,' I replied as I got to my feet. 'Essential.'

She nodded. 'Yeah, but there's something else.' I raised an eyebrow, wondering what could be more important than the key in my pocket. 'Don't you think it's significant that Grace was able to come into our reality and move the amulet in the first place?'

'Hell yes,' I said. Faith pressed her hand against my mouth and peered over her shoulder towards the dormitory. I took her hand away, 'Relax, no one can hear.'

She sighed. 'Still you shouldn't—'

'Yeah, yeah, whatever,' I said kneeling to pull another weed. Faith came down beside me as though she was getting ready to pray, a hurt expression on her face. I crushed the head of a dandelion between my fingers and cursed my abruptness. 'You're right,' I said, softening my voice. 'It *is* significant that Grace could move the amulet. It's another piece of the riddle. Now we need to work out how everything fits together.'

'How what riddle fits together, Miss Hopeful?'

A soft groan escaped Faith as we stood and faced Mary.

The Sister's favourite Consecrate was dazzling in her white uniform. Her long blonde hair was pulled back in a plait that hung over her shoulder. Her flat grey eyes regarded us.

'What'd you want?' I asked.

Faith sent me a cutting look and said, 'She means is there some way we can be of service to you, Mary?'

For a moment, I was tempted to make some remark about a free arse-kicking but I held my tongue. There were still riddles to solve and, until I knew everything I needed to know, I'd have to keep my mouth shut. 'Yep, that's what I meant. How can we help you, Mary?'

'What were you doing over at the Poinciana tree?'

I stared at her. *Think!* 'Umm we were taking a break. It's kind of hot out here,' I said. I waited for Faith to jump in with some brilliant excuse, since she'd been the bright spark all morning, but she said nothing.

Mary turned her eyes to the sky as though checking with God to see if I was telling the truth. Thankfully, He appeared to be on my side because she looked at Faith and smiled.

'I said, what were you doing over at the Poinciana?' *Damn.*

The silence grew. I could feel my heart speeding up; we were on dangerous ground, and still Faith let the seconds spin out. I couldn't stand it any longer. 'Look, Mary—'

'A young crow had fallen into the centre of the tree. We were rescuing it.'

I looked at Faith. *That's it? Great, we're screwed.*

'Rescuing a crow?' Mary asked.

'Yes,' Faith replied.

'You expect me to believe that?'

'We do good where we can. Crows belong to God too, you know.'

'So if I go over to the tree, I'll find a baby crow in a nest?'

'No. I said it was a *young* crow. It flew away.'

Mary's gaze passed between us, assessing. She knew Faith was lying her arse off but how could she prove it? She glanced at the Poinciana as though considering the value of making the trek over to check out Faith's story, and then she returned her steely gaze to us.

'Sister Merce said you have until lunch to finish the weeding up to the Church, so you'd better get a move on.'

'You're kidding?' Faith said, looking along the line of the fence all the way to the Church. I understood how she felt; it was a damn long way.

A smirk crossed Mary's face. 'I never kid about doing the Lord's work, Faith.' She raised her eyes heavenward before she looked at me again. 'I'll be watching you.'

Faith waited until the front door banged shut behind Mary before she collapsed on the grass, air rushing out of her lungs as though she'd been holding her breath for the last five minutes. 'Great, what now?'

I dropped down beside her, feeling the amulet press into my leg. I shuffled around on my butt so I was facing away from the buildings and took out the stone. Within its depths, swirls of blue and silver light blended together. I watched, fascinated.

'Hope?'

'Huh?'

'Did you hear me?'

I dragged my gaze away. 'Sorry, I was thinking. What did you say?'

'This isn't the time to get flaky, Hope.'

Like I don't know that. I brushed my finger over the stone in my hand and remembered my dream from the night before:

Grace and I were walking in the garden. 'What do

we do once we find the amulet?' I asked as we passed under the Poinciana. I thought we might stop at the stone seat (was this her way of providing a clue? Maybe; it seemed so obvious now that we had the amulet), but we walked on, passing the gymnasium as she talked.

'Draw the four virtues to hallowed ground, entice the Sister to follow. She will come, so will her cohort; too long have they practiced their vile ways to allow them to conceive of their destruction. But, they are weak in their pride and their vanity has blinded them to their vulnerability.'

We changed direction and wandered over to the Church. Silver-blue light bled through the stain glass windows and lit the darkened ground. It was beautiful.

'Vulnerability is good, but how do I draw the virtues?' I asked. 'What are they? What will happen if I draw them?'

Grace smiled. 'The amulet is the key.'

'I know that. Your diary told me that much – but look what happened when you and Charity tried to use it.'

'There were complications,' she replied, looping her arm through mine and leading me into the cemetery behind the church. We strolled between graves.

'No shit, and what makes you think this time will be any different?'

Grace sighed. 'Draw the four virtues.'

'Yes but how?'

'Caleb knows.'

'My Caleb?'

She was gone.

I sensed rather than felt Faith lean over my shoulder to touch the amulet. As her hand neared, a gentle vibration began deep within the stone as though in anticipation of the contact. Her fingertips came to rest against its smooth surface sending a warm flare up my arm and into my body before it was channelled into the earth beneath me. The vibration spread until everything around us seemed to pulse.

Suddenly, the voices inside my head rose up and I snapped my hand around the amulet, breaking contact with Faith. I shoved the amulet into my pocket and scrambled to my knees, dragging Faith with me, as I forced my hands to the task we'd been assigned.

Faith pulled the weeds with stiff, jerky movements as though she couldn't get her hands to move with their usual rhythm. 'Did you feel that?' she said.

I nodded. 'And we weren't the only ones.'

'Who else?'

'Merce.'

A moment later, the door to the dormitory slammed open. I knew it was the Sister without turning. I thought of Caleb. There was one more piece of the riddle to discover and it seemed he held the final clue. As the nun's shadow fell over us, I wondered how I could reach him.

Chapter Three

Have you ever had a moment of déjà vu, or divine inspiration, or unexpected warning? That's the knowledge inside me at work inside you. The difference between us is I remember the innate knowledge I was born with, but you – like almost every person who's left childhood behind – have forgotten. Don't feel bad. That's your blessing, while remembering is my curse.

Curse or not, I *know* we never really die; our spirit lives on for eternity. All the religions say so, although I know it at a deeper level than dogma. Yet, even though this knowledge is embedded in my mind, somehow, when it comes to Caleb, I'm like the rest of the human race: blind to the truth.

Grace tried to warn me that something had happened to Caleb, but the mind has a way of distorting things, of believing what hurts the least. And, although I'm privy to more knowledge than most, above everything else, I'm a girl – and like all girls, I can be as fragile as spun glass.

The Sunday my heart shattered started like any other.

5.00 am. I dressed in the dark, ignoring the girls around me. It was too early for pleasantries. Not that they'd be welcomed, or offered. Sister Anna Marie, sleepy as any of the girls, watched from the front of the room. Although the young nun was more relaxed than the other Sisters, the girls still moved with practiced silence, completing their tasks efficiently, knowing Sister Am (nice as she was) offered no protection from her less likeable Sisters. By 5.20 am, we were filing down the stairs in two straight rows, passing Merce and Sister Assumpta at the bottom.

The temptation to make some smart-arsed comment took hold of me but I held back. I still needed to conform since Merce and her crew were watching me like hawks. They knew something was going on; they sensed the riddle coming clearer and it made them nervous. I saw it in their faces and felt it in the uncomfortable glares that followed whenever I passed.

Then there was Faith, walking next to me, her eyes downcast but her tension rising like smoke from wet wood. It was so obvious to me and, I was sure, to the Sisters. After all, that's what they fed on: our fears.

I waited for Merce to pull someone out of the line but she let us pass without a word; morning Mass, it seemed, was too important to miss. Not for its redemptive qualities, of course, but appearances had to be maintained and Father Joachim was expecting us, which was fine with me. I'm not a particularly religious kind of girl – all that standing, sitting, kneeling is a pain in the arse – but going to Mass had benefits.

After weeks of constant vigilance, I needed some respite; a place where I could let down my guard without having to watch the Sisters. Father Joachim's church was exactly what I needed; a refuge where I could clear my head and try to work out the last part of the riddle.

As we left the dormitory, I peered through the branches of the trees, catching flashes of the church. I guess quaint would be the best way to describe the building, which was made from weatherboard painted brilliant white. A steeple with an iron bell that called us to Mass rose above the double doors, and was crowned with a cross. Shrubs of lush green grew beside the stairs, which lead inside where it was always peaceful.

The interior was rich with dark polished wood. Even the pews with the fold-down foot rests gleamed in the soft glow from the flickering yellow lamps lining the walls, while above us, wooden beams criss-crossed the ceiling like petrified spider webs. And everywhere was the gentle face of Jesus, looking over his flock of wayward girls.

At the front of the church was the Sanctuary with its marble altar – the only extravagance – covered by the Vestments. Behind the altar and to the left was the Table of Oblation, which had a candelabra with seven arms, a golden chalice and plate for the Sacraments. Resting on the edge of the Table was Father Joachim's Bible, its red page marker twisting in the breeze caused by the priest as he readied the Sanctuary for the Mass. He had no altar boys to help him; they were as forbidden here as we were in their world.

Behind the altar was a wooden cross with gold nails and a gold plate with the letters INRI engraved on it, but there were no suffering effigies of Christ to be seen anywhere in the church. I asked Father Joachim about that one day after Mass.

'We know Jesus suffered horribly and died for us,' he said, his voice warm and rich like the wooden pew he polished with tender care. 'That is not what we need reminding of; it is the reason for his suffering and sacrifice that we must remember.' He stopped polishing and looked at me.

I glanced around the church, at the paintings and statues of Jesus, each one a dedication to benevolence and compassion. 'Love,' I said.

'Indeed,' Father Joachim replied, continuing his

polishing. 'It's the only thing that can save us.'

The girls were quiet as we marched over to the church, the crunching of our feet on the gravel and the cawing crows the only sounds imposing on the overcast morning. The mood lightened inside the church, its warmth and invitation working their magic as we lingered in the Narthex.

While I waited for the other girls to dip their fingers into the Holy Water, I thought about the penitents who'd been here before us, never allowed to enter any further into the church and excluded from the Communion because of their 'sins'. *Where was the compassion and love for them?* I wondered dipping my fingers into the water and touching my forehead, chest and shoulders. I sat at the back of the church, beneath a painting of Jesus the Shepherd; his lean, bearded face peaceful as he gazed across the distance hills, while his flock milled at his feet. In the soft light from the lamp, he reminded me of Caleb.

Father Joachim appeared in the Sanctuary, dressed in flowing green and gold robes, a serious but kind expression on his face as he looked over his congregation. 'In the name of the Father,' he began, and I switched to autopilot until he reached the Liturgy, where I zoned out completely.

I stared up at the picture of Jesus as my mind drifted to the amulet. I knew the stone was powerful. I'd learnt that much from Grace's diary, but no matter how I turned the riddle of its existence over in my mind, I just couldn't seem to make the connections. The amulet was a key but to what? It was a weapon, but how did it work? It was a lodestone, but what did it draw? I sighed and focused on the benign face of the Shepherd.

Jesus moved.

Stepped out of the painting.

Sat down beside me and took my hand.

His face changed; the eyes from brown to blue, the lips fuller, the beard receding until I was looking at Caleb.

Caleb?

'Hey Dao-Girl, what's happening?' he said. I looked around the church, panic tingling in every nerve. 'Relax, they can't see me.'

'How can this be?' I asked, and he pressed his mouth to mine. I closed my eyes, losing myself in the pressure of his lips, forgetting everything: the Sisterhood, Faith, Grace and Charity, the unavenged penitents.

I could have stayed in that moment forever, but Caleb had other ideas. He pulled away and took my hands in his own. 'If there is to be grace in the world, you must act now. You can't turn from this, and they grow more powerful the longer you wait.'

Hurt by the accusation I heard in his voice, I turned towards Father Joachim. 'I can't act until I have all the pieces of the riddle.'

Caleb touched my face, urging me to look at him again. 'All the knowledge you need to draw the four Virtues is within your reach: rock, book, home.'

'What does that mean?' I demanded. There was something wrong here, something dancing on the edge of my mind.

'The answer, and all the strength you will ever need, is within you,' Caleb said. His voice had a floating quality, and when I looked into his eyes, the pupils seeped blackness into the blue of his irises.

Fear settled over my heart. 'Caleb? Why are you here? What's going on?'

His smile was sky-wide and as just beautiful. 'Resurrection, babe.'

'What? I don't understand—'

'It's been a buzz seeing you, Dao-girl. I hope we meet again soon.'

'No.' I gripped his hands, trying to hold him to me.

He shook his head, a soft negation of what I wanted. 'No point resisting, you know the Way,' he said as the blackness engulfed him. 'I love you.'

'No!'

'Hope? Snap out of it, we've got to go up for Communion,' Faith muttered.

I slumped against her and she squeezed my arm, a warning in her grip. I nodded and shook off her hand as I looked at the painting. Jesus had returned to his quiet contemplation. A soft sob escaped my throat. The girls around me flicked curious looks my way as we stood and filed out of the pews, forming two rows that shuffled towards Father Joachim. Sister Am, her pale brow creased with a frown, raised a finger to her lips, demanding silence.

Not that I cared. I wanted to shout and rage at the unfairness and cruelty of it all. *What right did Jesus have to look so serene when sacrifices were being made? How much more blood needed to be spilled before this would end?*

'The Lamb of God.'

Father Joachim's voice cut across my thoughts and I blinked away the tears that threatened to fall. *Was that what Caleb had become?* I drew a shuddering breath and concentrated on the back of Faith's shoes as we drew closer to the priest. I needed time to think about the vision, about Caleb's message, about his—

No! My mind shied away from the thought.

'The Lamb of God.'

The soft jingling of metal drew my attention. Mary was watching me from the first pew, the rosary running through her fingers. I could read the curiosity in her face and the cold sense of duty behind her expression.

She wanted to know what was wrong. The eyes of the Sisters were everywhere.

Faith dropped to one knee, raising her head towards Father Joachim, who placed a white wafer on her tongue. She stood, made the sign of the cross, bowed her head at the altar before joining the line of girls moving back to their seats. I followed her example.

'The Body of Caleb.'

Startled, I raised my eyes to Father Joachim, who traced the sign of the Cross on my forehead before placing the Eucharist in my mouth. He gave me a small dismissive nod, his attention shifting to the girl behind me. *Had I heard him right?* I lurched to my feet, glancing at the other girls to see if they had heard the priest. Each one, including Mary, had her head bowed in prayer. *Another vision? What does it mean?*

Somehow, I got to my seat and slid onto my knees, pressing my forehead against my folded hands. There were no prayers to offer, just a swirl of confusion. I waited, concentrating on my breathing, slowing my thoughts. Beside me, Faith murmured the *Hail Mary*, the rhythm of her intonation calming my mind.

Address one problem at a time, I told myself. *Break it down into smaller components.*

A breath in.

Caleb? No, can't deal with that yet.

An exhalation.

What about the clues he gave: rock, book, home?

Breath—

Something clicked. I lifted my head from my hands, my heart speeding up as it fired with excitement. *That's it! The diary. The amulet. The penitents. The Sisters.* Like the links in a riddle revealed, the whole became clear. I wanted to shout. I wanted to hug Faith. I wanted to confront Merce, to shove my finger in her face and shout, 'Fuck you.'

Caleb was right. It was time to bring the Sisterhood to an end.

Caleb.

His name was like an electric shock. I shivered, not wanting to face what his visitation could mean. My mind veered away, latching onto the task ahead. Defeating the Sisterhood would be dangerous, maybe even deadly, but it would be a whole lot less painful than considering a world without Caleb.

Chapter Four

Each of us has a voice inside that's meant to guide us through our lives. Some call this voice instinct, some call it their consciousness. Others think it's God, or the Devil, depending on their internal landscape. It doesn't matter what that voice is called. What's important is listening when it starts muttering that something's wrong. When that happens, I'm all ears.

Almost three weeks past before that voice fell silent. My little performance (as Faith put it) during Mass had been reported to Merce. The nun stalked me like a starved wolf for a week, until one of the girls – a runaway called Leah – was caught fraternising with some weedy, pimple-faced delivery guy who she wouldn't have noticed in the real world. So stupid.

For Merce and her horde, Leah's indiscretion was the perfect opportunity to teach the girls about the 'ramifications of immoral behaviour'. The nun took out her trusty scissors, gloating as Leah's blonde curls floated to the floor, before dragging the sobbing girl down to her office for some 'further disciplinary action'. I heard Caleb's words in my head as I waited for Leah to return: *They grow more powerful the longer you wait.* Her bed remained empty.

The episode with Leah didn't get me completely off the hook. There was still Mary and her Consecrates to avoid, which I did by keeping a low profile and staying away from Faith as much as possible – not an easy thing to do when I had a secret that I felt like blurting out every time I saw her. Then there was the amulet; a constant reminder of what needed to be done.

My frustration grew during the first two weeks but I controlled it, waited, and soon the Consecrates got tired of their watching. When I sensed their attention drifting to other things, I sidled up to Faith and whispered for her to meet me in the attic that night.

She listens, eyes fixed on my face, while I explain Caleb's visitation in the church, the purpose of the diary and amulet, and about getting the Sisters to Father Joachim's church. When I'm finished, I try to answer her questions but the voices in my mind distract me with an urgent whisper.

Not now, I respond, shutting them out.

The attic window frames Faith. Behind her, the Poinciana in the garden stretches out its limbs, obscuring the church from view. For once, there isn't a crow to be seen, which is strange, but their absence catches only a flicker of my attention as I focus on trying to convince Faith that I know the answer to our riddle.

'Do you understand what I'm telling you? If we take the diary and this,' I hold out the amulet, 'over to the—'

I almost miss the soft scrape behind me but I see the widening of Faith's eyes as she glances over my shoulder. A sinking feeling fills my stomach as I turn. There are three of them: Mary, out the front; Patience, a step behind and Gertie, filling the stairwell.

'Well, look at this, girls. There's a couple of rats in the attic.'

Patience giggles as she steps to Mary's side. Gertie stays where she is, blocking our escape. Mary flicks her eyes towards Patience, whose smile shrivels at the blistering look Mary delivers.

I watch her approach, wary as a mongoose with a cobra. I hear Faith's rapid breathing. Mary stops in front of me. I don't move or speak; I wait for her to show me what comes next. If there was ever a chance for Faith and I to get out of confronting the Sisterhood, Mary's presence in the attic strips it away. One way or the other, we are locked in.

When Mary chooses our path, things happen fast.

'What have we here?' she asks, reaching for the diary.

I block her hand with my arm, pulling the diary away, but she comes closer, her body pressing against mine as we struggle. There's movement behind me and I sense Patience and Gertie crossing the floor.

'Shit,' Faith mutters, stepping between the twins and me even though she doesn't stand a chance.

Mary's beautiful face is close to mine. I can see her long dark eyelashes, the tiny freckles on her nose, the fine hairs along the curve of her cheek like the fuzz on a fresh peach, the red bow of her lips. I put my hand against her chest, pushing her away again. She resists, gripping my wrist, as she swing us around so that her back is to the window and mine is touching Faith, who is trying to keep Patience and Gertie at bay.

'Get the fuck out of the way, whore,' Gertie says.

Patience adds her own chant. 'Bitch, bitch, bitch,' she says, reaching past Faith to snag my nightdress.

Whore? Bitch? The Sister' would be pleased, I think, fighting nervous laughter as I shrug Patience off with one arm and strain against Mary with the other; not an easy thing to do because she is pulling on the diary.

Resistance is futile, Dao-girl.

I listen and— relax. Mary staggers closer to the window. The diary begins to slide from my fingers. Triumph streaks across her face as she regains her balance and doubles her efforts.

Faith's hand slips into mine, the one clasping the amulet. The stone lays cold between Faith and I for an instant, then it flares like a sun-lit diamond filling the attic with a light so pure I'm sure I've been struck blind.

I hear rather than see what happened next: Gertie and Patience stumble, cursing, as they call out to Mary, who suddenly releases the diary. Her foot bangs against the skirting board and I feel her hand flutter against my face for a second before the window shatters. I reach for her, breaking contact with Faith and the amulet. Darkness descends as Mary screams, an unwinding of her final breath that is cut off with the sickening thud of her body on the pathway below.

Silence follows. I look at Faith, her mouth is open, her eyes blank with shock. A breeze creeps through the broken window. She grimaces as though she's been touched by the Devil himself. Behind her, the Consecrates are moving towards the attic stairs. Patience is crying but Gertie is dry-eyed as she half drags, half carries her sister out of the attic.

Gertie's urgency is infectious and I grab Faith by the arm but she refuses to move. Instead, she points to the window – *as if I didn't know* – and tears spill down her cheeks.

'I know,' I say, 'but what's done is done.'

'Hope!'

I shake my head. Although I never liked Mary, not for a second, I didn't want this to happen. 'Mourn her later,' I explain, leading Faith to the stairs. 'We have to go.'

The dormitory is in chaos. The girls are gathered around Gertie, who stands on her bed telling them about Mary, and the attic, and the light.

We're almost at the door when the Consecrate sees us.

'They did it,' she yells, pointing.

I turn to face her.

There's a psychological condition I read about once, where people who've been abused come to rely on their abuser, even defending them when the situation comes out in the open. It's almost like they come to love the pain and fear, but really it's that the abused knows the boundaries, and how far they can push before they get fucked over again. Looking into the faces of the girls in the dormitory, I realise that, for all of their hatred and fear of the Sisters, they didn't want their boundaries broken— and that made Faith and I the enemy.

I brace myself for their assault but Faith pulls on my hand, drawing my attention to the obvious. 'Sister Constance is gone,' she says. That can mean only one thing; the doddering nun has gone to get Merce.

We run and the girls come after us, crashing down the stairs that we leap by twos and threes. At the bottom, we encounter Merce. There's a second of hesitation, as though Faith and I are caught in the slow-motion of a nightmare. The nun's eyes flare with silver streaks and I grab Faith's hand, barrelling into Merce, my shoulder going numb as it connects with her breastbone. She grunts, her fingers scratching at my shoulder as she crashes to the floor.

The pounding of feet behind us slows. I glance over my shoulder and catch the stunned expressions on the girls' faces as they see the invincible Merce lying on her back, habit hitched up to show chubby alabaster legs, flailing against the indignity of their exposure. The sight is almost comic.

Faith and I race through the front door but pull up short, any thought of laughter gone. Mary's twisted body lies across the path, her blood filling the cracks between the pavers. Her head is turned towards the dormitory, her eyes open, as though she's watching for her friends to come out and play.

'Get off me!' Merce's roar breaks the moment. Faith and I bolt for the church as pandemonium spills out of the dormitory.

Where have the crows gone? I wonder as I hear Merce calling to Sister Assumpta and Sister Anslem. 'Deal with this mess,' she orders. The words are harsh and I wince, remembering how Mary had served the Sisters and lost whatever was sweet about her in the process. Wherever she is now, I hope she can't hear those words.

We reach the fence surrounding the church and I turn. Merce is stalking after us, moving fast but not running. Her eyes lock onto mine and a sudden heaviness invades my limbs.

Faith tugs on my arm, trying to drag me up the steps to the church. 'Come on, Hope. We're almost there,' she says.

I can't move. There is a strange pulling in my chest. I glance down; a silver-blue stream of light is flowing from my body. In my hand, the amulet vibrates in quick, urgent bursts, but it isn't enough to dam the river of energy being drawn from me.

Faith sighs and, with an effort, I turn my head towards her. A twin stream of light erupts from her chest and merges with mine. I follow the light with my eyes to where Merce stands, drawing the stream into her mouth.

The scene is surreal and I'm suddenly reminded of a painting by Victor Brauner that I'd seen... somewhere; thinking is becoming a problem as the light flows from me. The painting is called *Le ver luisant*, which translates as... *The Glow Worm*. As Merce sucks the willpower from me, I wonder if Brauner had seen the Sister in action because, it seems to me, she is the ugly worm of his work.

Sleepiness seeps into my bones, filling them with wet cement. I ache and throb as my living essence flows into Merce. Beside me, Faith lets out a moaning yawn and sinks towards the ground.

We are lost.

'What's going on out here?' Father Joachim asks, his robes swishing as he comes down the stairs. He walks past me, his hand briefly touching my elbow, and stands between Merce and us. Suddenly the silver stream turns, flows around Father Joachim and back to me, filling my limbs, my heart, my mind until I feel as jittery as a firefly. Faith shudders.

'I asked a question, Sister.'

'I didn't know you were on the grounds this evening Father,' Merce replies, her voice almost humble as she presses her hands together and bends her head in a gesture of supplication.

Father Joachim isn't fooled. 'For the last time, Sister, what is going on?' he demands, looking over her shoulder to the dormitory. 'What are the girls doing out of bed and why are they crying?'

'Mary fell through the attic window, Father,' I say.

Merce glares at me.

'Oh my Lord! Is she alright?'

'She's dead, Father.'

'God in Heaven,' he says, making the sign of the cross.

'Actually, we haven't established that, Father Joachim,' Merce says, hijacking the conversation. 'There has been an accident and one of the girls is hurt, but my Sisters are attending to her. Unfortunately, these two wayward souls have caused a bit of a ruckus tonight and stirred up the whole dormitory, before apparently deciding to run away from the consequences of their actions.' Merce takes Faith by the arm. 'However, as always, we will return them to the righteous path, Father.'

How convincing she sounds. Even I almost believe it's Faith and I who are in the wrong. I look at the priest, his face is clouded with doubt as he glances from us to Merce, then to his church, and I realise something as I watch his internal battle. He knows about them; about the Sisters and what they do at St Mary's, or at least he has an idea, and he's turned a blind eye. My heart sinks; there'd be no help from him.

Merce knows it too. 'But please, Father, you mustn't concern yourself with the activities of our girls. God's work is surely beyond these trifling matters.'

A frown slips across the priest's brow and his face hardens with resolve. 'There is no matter too small for God's attention, Sister,' he says, stepping between the nun and Faith, breaking her hold. Fury fills Merce's face as he takes her arm and propels her towards the dormitory. He glances over his shoulder as he draws her away. 'You two wait in the Church until I return.'

I nod but I can tell from the bleak set of his mouth that returning isn't something he believes he'll be doing any time soon. Merce also looks back at us. There's no disguising the murderous glint in her eyes. I say a silent prayer for Father Joachim as I take Faith's hand and climb the steps into the church.

Closing the doors behind Faith, I rest my forehead against the wood and twist the lock. Not because I believe it'll keep the Sisters out when they come for us, but because it gives me some comfort to hear the tumblers fall into place. I wait a moment longer, letting the peace of the church settle over me before I follow Faith into the Nave. She reaches the first pew, where she genuflects. I follow her lead and then sit next to her, putting the diary and the amulet between us. She glances at them before turning her gaze to the Cross behind the altar.

'What now?' she asks.

I don't answer straight away because the voices are murmuring in my head. I wait for one to come through clearly. When she does, I hesitate, unsure if I can say what she tells me out loud in a church. It seems like sacrilege. I shift in the pew and Faith looks at me.

'Well?'

I close my eyes for a second, open them again. 'We brew a little magic,' I say, and wait for the lightning bolt.

Chapter Five

A man's scream – *Father Joachim!* – comes from the direction of the dormitory. Faith looks at me, her pale face tight with fear. 'Was that?'

'I think so.'

'What do we do?'

The amulet is cold and dark when I pick it up. I turn the stone over, feeling its weight grow with my sense of responsibility. *Am I strong enough to do what is needed?* I lift the diary from the pew and hear Grace's voice in my mind.

Surrender.

I hold my hand out to Faith. Her fingers close around mine; the amulet presses into our palms and begins to warm. 'What's going to happen?' she asks.

'Don't worry, you'll be okay,' I say, although I know it might not be true. 'Hold onto the diary, close your eyes and focus on me.'

'But— '

'No more questions, Faith,' I say, closing my eyes.

As soon as Faith touches the diary, I feel a vibration beneath my fingers. The tremor increases, spreading up my arm and through my body. The rhythm changes, speeds up until it matches the beat of my heart. Power surges through my veins and seems to pulse against my skin before breaking through, reverberating outward from me into the air.

The voices in my head sing as though this was the moment they've been waiting for; a choir of angels reaching a crescendo not meant to be heard by a mere mortal. I bite my lip and pray for the sound to end.

Silence.

I open my eyes. The church is bathed in silver-blue light. The walls, the ceiling, the floor glow with brilliance. Every mundane object – the nails holding the pews together, the plastic numbers on the hymn board, the lead cames in the stain glass windows – is beautiful. A moth flutters above my head, trailing silver ribbons from the tips of its wings. I smile and look at Faith.

Her face is a mask of terror.

In my delight, I've forgotten Faith is used to only one reality; the one she's been locked into by her parents, by her schooling, by her culture. Overwhelmed, she wants to run and hide. I see it in the set of her face, that desperate instinct to flee the unknown, but fleeing isn't an option and I tug on her hand, without breaking contact, bringing her attention to me. Her eyes are *anime* perfect: large, glassy; ready to shatter.

'Breathe and focus,' I say and her eyes close. I know what she's doing – trying to escape. I shake her hand again and her eyes snap open. 'Breathe and focus,' I demand.

This time she locks her gaze to mine and I note the steady rise and fall of her chest as the lines of concentration appear between her eyebrows. My breathing falls into rhythm with hers. Between our palms, the amulet pulses with the same regularity and the air resonates as though the entire church – maybe the entire planet – has synchronised with our breathing.

That's when I feel them. Grace and Charity. The virtues.

I don't know what I expected from this moment; some sort of big-band fanfare, fireworks maybe, but it's not like that. They just... arrive. There's a swirl of dust, a gathering of particles, and two girls dressed in dark grey uniforms with starched white aprons materialise beside the altar. The silver-blue light is drawn towards them, adding power to their substance, before fading, leaving the church once again lit by lamplight.

The soft glow can't disguise the thinness of their faces, nor the hollows beneath their eyes. Bonnets cover their heads. This makes me curious; is their hair tucked away or have they suffered the humiliation of having their heads shaved?

Then, as though reading my mind, Grace pulls the bonnet from her head and a spill of dark hair falls across her shoulders. The gesture is defiant and is met by a scream from beyond the church: long, inhuman. Faith twists towards the door, breaking the connection between us. The diary falls to the pew with a dull thud and, as the heat goes out of the amulet, I slip it into my pocket. There is a pause and the cry comes again, followed by a chorus of responses.

Faith looks at me. 'The crows?'

I watch the girls, waiting for them to vanish but they only waver for a moment, like heatwaves over a sun-baked road, then Grace's jaw clenches with determination and she comes more fully into being. She touches Charity's elbow and I see the smaller girl flinch. Her form flickers as her eyes dart around the church, as though searching for a way to escape.

I know how you feel, I think.

Grace murmurs, perhaps a word of encouragement, and Charity is with us, as real as Faith or me. She glances around before following Grace down the altar steps. I stand beside Faith, ready to meet them.

The moment is weird. We're like allies with a common cause, fighting on different fronts, but we're strangers too. We're shy and uncertain; what are we supposed to do, now that we're here, together?

Here together? I wonder. *Where exactly is 'here'?* This is an interesting riddle, one that steals my attention. Something has changed but I'm not sure what it is. I send my senses in search of an answer. They are drawn to the church doors. Around and beneath them, dripping through the cracks and pooling in the gap at the bottom, are deep shadows. There is something terrible about them and, as I watch, they seep further into the church. I feel touched by coldness, polluted, and I shudder.

'What do you see, Hope?'

The sound of Grace's voice pulls me back into my body. 'Something's different,' I say.

'What do you mean?' Faith asks.

'I don't think we're in Kansas anymore, Dorothy.'

'What?'

'Never mind.' I glance at the sludge pushing under the doors. 'We're running out of time. Do you feel that?' I ask the question of Grace.

'Yes, I do.'

'They're coming.'

'I know.'

'Let's go then.'

Grace smiles. 'My mother used to say, "Patience is the better part of valour." Perhaps we should collect our thoughts and devise a plan before we go rushing headlong into the dangers we must face? There is, after all, no point to idle sacrifice.'

'How noble. If only you had that opinion before you cast me to the Sisters.'

It is said softly but its impact is like a sledgehammer. We turn to Charity, who has retreated to the altar steps and is looking at Grace with bright anger.

'I did what I thought was best,' Grace says.

'For whom was it best? Not for *me*, that is certain.'

'You knew there were risks.'

'Perhaps. But you hid the limit of your knowledge in your eagerness to escape the Sisters, even though you knew it would be the end of me.'

'I knew nothing of the sort,' Grace replies.

I exchange a glance with Faith, the words from the diary fresh in my mind: *Of Charity laying lifeless at the edge of a black lake.*

'You betrayed me,' Charity says.

'I could say the same of you.' As she speaks, Grace glides towards Charity, her movement fluid, ghostly.

I sense no threat, but Charity steps backwards until she's standing next to the altar. 'I betrayed no one,' she says.

'Really? And what of the time you spent in Sister Merce's office? Just what were you telling the Sisters?' Grace asks, drawing closer.

'Do you think I had a choice to be there?' Charity places a hand on the altar, its solidness seems to fortify her. She holds her ground, gazing down at Grace.

'You had a choice about what you revealed.'

'I revealed nothing. I *resisted* them because I trusted you. And how did you repay my trust? You lead me into that office knowing we didn't have the power to defeat them,' Charity says. Tears glitter in her eyes. 'You sacrificed me so you could escape the Sisterhood.'

'Is that so? You forget, my life was forfeited that day as well.'

'Dying by your own hand is hardly the same as being thrown to the wolves. What is it you said about the girls who drank bleach? It is the coward's path?'

Silence fills the church. Grace and Charity stare at each other over the altar. Faith is struck dumb. My own inner voices are mute. No sound comes from beyond or within the church. It's up to me to break the impasse.

'What the *fuck*?'

'Hope!'

'What? You heard Charity,' I say, pointing to Grace. 'She killed herself.'

'It changes nothing,' Grace says.

'Like hell it doesn't. I've been listening to you my whole life, following your guidance and all this time you've been hiding the truth from me.'

'Would you stop yelling. You're in a church.'

'Please listen to Faith,' Charity says.

'I think you girls are missing the bigger picture here,' I say, pointing to the door behind me. 'The Sisters are out there, ready to do God only knows what to us, and the one thing we had going for us was that we were all trying to accomplish the same thing. Now it seems at least one of us has her own agenda.'

Grace turns towards me. 'My agenda, as you call it, has been escaping the Sisterhood and, to achieve that, sacrifices had to be made.'

'So you admit the deed?' Charity says, coming down from the altar.

'I'm sorry for what happened to you,' Grace replies, taking Charity's hands, 'but in the greater scheme of things, my actions make little difference. We needed to be with these two, and we are. Forget what has gone before, Charity, and deal with now. Believe in me, trust me, for it is the only way we can succeed at the task laid before us.' She turns her impassioned gaze to me. 'As for you, perhaps you should listen to the voices within; their wisdom is boundless.'

As though in agreement, the voices in my mind decide it's time to start expressing their opinion; they begin with a whisper but quickly build to a shout. With an effort, I turn them down and look at Grace, who nods as though she can hear them too.

I shake my head as I waver between reluctance and acceptance. Trusting in Grace has been part of my inner life for so long that I feel adrift with the revelation of her suicide. Why didn't she make a stand against the Sisters? What about honour and courage?

'I'm not sure I can do what you ask,' I say.

'You would ignore my guidance because of this admission?' Grace asks.

I falter. 'I just can't— '

'Look, all of this is very interesting,' Faith interrupts, 'but don't you think we have a bigger problem? The Sisters? Remember? You can argue over who did what later, now we have to do something constructive.'

Grace turns to Faith. 'You're right, but first we must plan our next step. We can't afford any more mistakes.' She glances at Charity, who gives her a tentative nod.

'We don't have the time, we need to act now,' Faith says.

Grace looks at Faith, steady and uncompromising. 'The Sisters will come when we are ready,' she says.

'You're wrong,' I say. The voices in my mind are clamouring for attention: *the Sisters are coming, the Sisters are coming,* they wail. I focus my awareness, sending it beyond the church doors, into the darkness.

The voices are right.

Chapter Six

Intuition becomes reality as I step through the church doors. I recognise the landscape, though it looks nothing like the St Mary's I know. In the distance, jagged mountains pierce a black sky littered with sharp silver stars. There is the hint of a river between a slash in the peaks. Trees march across low-slung fields of dark earth until they reach the perimeter fence of the school, where they are stopped dead in their advance. I recognise the gymnasium and the dormitory, the convent and the school building, the Poinciana tree and the seat beneath it.

All of the elements that make up life at the convent are here but different because they are submerged beneath a black sea of feathered bodies. As far as I can see, crows perch, silent as the moment before a scream.

'Oh,' Faith murmurs as the girls join me on the top step of the church.

'The midnight princes,' Charity says, stepping down onto the next stair.

The birds accommodate her by shuffling backwards, making room, though they remain silent. A bizarre urge grips me: I want to race through them, howling like a kid at the beach chasing seagulls, just to hear them squawk and to watch them fly.

Grace puts a restraining hand on my arm. 'Not a good idea.'

I nod as a protesting groan draws my attention to the church. Like the rest of the landscape, it's covered with birds. Crows congregate on every shingle, gutter and windowsill. They perch on the cross above the steeple and crowd into the belfry, their clawed feet clicking and scraping as they jostled for space.

The crows, though, are the least of our problems.

'Well, well, well, what have we here?' Merce's voice floats out of the darkness from somewhere near the Poinciana. 'What clever little girls we have at St Mary's. Wicked, deceitful, ungrateful little girls, but clever nonetheless.' I hear a snicker and know she isn't alone; her Sisters are with her.

'And what a feat they have accomplished. A whole new level of reality. Impressive. Did they learn that from you in Physics, Sister Assumpta?'

'Not from I, Sister,' comes the reply.

'But, lo, not only have they manipulated the laws of time and space, my Sisters,' Merce continues as though the fat nun hadn't spoken, 'they have managed to resurrect the dead. Is that really you, Grace? And your little novice, Charity? Funny, I distinctly remember killing her.'

'I remember too, Sister,' Charity says, as Grace steps down beside her and reaches for her hand. For a moment, Charity draws away, as though reluctant to feel her touch.

I catch my breath. *Not now Charity. We need you.*

She glances my way and allows Grace to capture her fingers. Together, the girls descend another step, causing the crows to flap into the air before settling again.

'And now it's time to do unto you as you have done unto us,' Grace says.

A snort comes out of the dark beneath the Poinciana. 'Is that right, child?'

'Yes,' Grace replies.

The simple conviction in Grace's statement fills me with a kind of dread. How can she be so sure the time is right to face the Sisters? Is it because she'd already died once and so doesn't fear what the Sisters could do? I know our spirits are eternal, but I still don't want to give up my human existence, not yet. And, how does Grace even know we can do anything to defeat the Sisters anyway? Jesus, I don't have a fucking clue what to do next. We are in this place – wherever this is – with two dead girls and a Sisterhood of freaks, and Grace is making this encounter sound like we're catching up for ice-cream on a sunny Sunday afternoon.

My heart crashes against my ribs as the doubts invade in my head. I know where they're coming from: Merce. I feel the nun pushing into my mind and, though I try to get her out, the panic deepens. The urge to crawl back into the church and hide washes over me.

Be at peace, Hope.

Charity's voice – clear, sweet and unexpected – breaks through the panic, bringing calm. I send her a grateful smile

Merce chuckles as she withdraws from my mind. 'Why don't you show yourself, you old witch?' I say.

'In due course,' the nun replies.

Beside me, Faith lets out a shuddering breath. I take her hand. 'You okay?'

'Sister Merce was talking to me,' Faith says, touching her temple. 'She said we couldn't beat them, that we were stupid to even try.' Tears fill her eyes as she looks at Grace and Charity, and then at me. 'And I believed her.'

'Just another trick,' Grace says. 'You'll know it if she tries it again.'

'She's so damn strong,' Faith says, and I squeeze

her finger.

'We're stronger,' I say, as a long, low caw and the flutter of wings tells me the Sisters are on the move.

'What's going to happen?' Charity asks.

'Damned if I know,' I reply, feeling the tension break within me. After months of waiting, the time has finally come for action.

From beneath the Poinciana tree, the Sisters come.

The crows take flight, screeching as they fly into the air, revealing the Sisters racing across the lawn. I can't take my eyes off them. They move with a deadly fluidity, silver light glowing in their eyes as they close the distance between us. 'I told you they weren't human,' Faith says.

The Sisters cross the driveway and I can hear the scattering of gravel beneath their feet. I bat away a warm, feathered body that flashes past my head as I identify the nuns. Sister Patrice is racing in from the right, next to her is Sister Assumpta who, despite the layers of fat, moves with frightening speed. Sisters Adrian and Anslem are closing fast on the left and, leading through the centre is Merce.

I quiver at the sight of her; our enemy unmasked.

Not that the nun *looks* different. Her face is set with the same cruel self-importance, the cold eyes are slit with the same determination, the mouth is still held in a sneer of contempt. No, it's something more fundamental beneath the mask; a wound ripped open to reveal the centuries old malevolence that corrupts her soul.

Unclean.

Unnatural.

Unworldly

The words whisper across my mind as the nuns reach the edge of the church grounds. I stumble back-

199

wards up the steps, the girls following me as we try to put some distance between the Sisterhood and us.

'What were we thinking?' Faith says. I can barely hear her over the cawing of the crows that swoop and swirl above us.

'Don't worry,' Charity yells, though her voice wavers with fear. 'This is consecrated ground, they won't be able—'

Merce crashes through the gate and the other nuns run in behind her. Eight metres and they'll be on us. We retreat further, pressing up against the church doors, but it's pointless.

The savage gleam in Merce's eyes tells me she agrees: *I warned you, child.*

I'm distracted from the menacing whisper in my head by Grace. 'The amulet,' she says.

I shake my head. 'Not going to do us any good.'

'Live up to the name they gave you, Hope,' Grace responds.

'Fine,' I mutter as I reach into my pocket and wrap my fingers around the stone. I turn to face the nuns who are only a few metres away and call on the voices in my head to help me. Faith, Charity and Grace huddle behind me as I hold up the amulet but it remains cold and useless. Fear closes over my heart.

Merce lets out a triumphant howl and the crows that have settled over the church suddenly take flight, lifting like a dark shroud, revealing a brilliant silver-blue light that floods from the church in streams. The light hits the nuns. Sister Anslem first, right in the chest. She explodes into flame, dancing for a moment before falling in a smouldering heap. A second later, Sister Assumpta is consumed, her fat body twisting and sizzling where it falls. Sister Adrian whimpers as she turns and runs for the gate; a bolt takes her in the back and passes through her, engulfing the Poinciana tree. Another bolt crackles towards Merce.

The nun moves fast; faster than I thought possible. Her arm whips out and drags Sister Patrice into the line of fire. As the light strikes the nun, it flings them both backwards, but only Sister Patrice is swallowed by the flame. She crackles and spits as the inferno takes her. I shudder as I see the look on her face; she's smiling with relief.

Merce rolls and comes up running, moving away from us, back into the night. The silvery light fades to a passive milky-blue, then disappears as the crows settle over the church again.

Merce's voice rips through the darkness again. 'Evil, wicked girls. Jezebels, all of you. Oh, look what you have done to my sisters. Dirty sinners. You will die for this.' Her voice is like a swarm of angry wasps; filled with venom. I put my hands over my ears, wanting to block her out but she's in my mind, jabbing at my brain.

'You think you are so clever, so strong, so good and righteous. What gives *you* the right to decimate my sisterhood? By what authority do *you* act? I am the authority here.'

The sting of her voice drives me down the stairs and I'm barely aware of the girls as they stumble with me, as though the nun's words have wrapped around us like a noose. We shuffle along the path and, as we reach the shattered gate, the crows once again take to the air. They circle above us; a swirling mass of judgement. I tear my eyes away from the birds and focus on trying to get Merce out of my head. Her grip is strong and the more I struggle, the more the noose tightens.

Yield and overcome.

The command comes from deep inside my mind, a single male voice, rising above the rest, and I turn towards the voice as Merce's tirade rolls on.

'Harlots and whores. Do you think God is on your side? Do you think He will protect you? Huh! Why would He when you are less than a speck of dust? You are alone, powerless, worthless, nothing. *Mine* to dispose of as I please.'

I hear Faith gasp as Merce utters these last words and I look up, expecting to see all my nightmares made flesh. Instead, the figure that steps out from behind the split trunk of the Poinciana is almost fragile. Her habit is dishevelled and one knee-high stocking is gathered around an ankle. Strands of hair brush her face, softening it.

Yield and overcome.

The voice is louder, insistent, and I frown, distracted. What harm is there in the bedraggled woman before us?

'Don't be fooled,' Grace says. She points at Merce, her finger as straight and steady as a dagger. 'Your disguise will not work. We've seen you for what you are.'

Merce sighs with the long-suffering patience of a saint and clasps her hands to her chest, but a smirk plays across her mouth as she says, 'That was always your problem, Grace. You never knew when to keep your mouth shut. It will be a pleasure to kill you.'

'I'm not afraid of you,' Grace replies.

The voice whispers again: *That's not true.*

Caleb?

No.

Patrick?

Yes. Grace must yield to overcome; it is the only way.

I reach for Grace, tag the sleeve of her dress but she yanks her arm free and locks her eyes onto mine. I shiver; they are as empty as a broken promise.

'Don't interfere,' she says.

She takes a deliberate step towards Merce and, as she does, I feel the power pulling me towards the nun wane. A smile of satisfaction settles across the Sister's face as Grace crosses the driveway, closing the last few metres between them until they stand almost toe to toe beneath the branches of the Poinciana.

'What the hell is she doing,' Faith asks.

'I'm not sure,' I reply, taking her hand as I reach for Charity. Faith's eyes widen as the amulet flares between our palms. Warmth shoots through my body and into the girls holding my hands. Our minds touch and I feel their doubt. 'But we have to believe in her,' I say.

My eyes are drawn to the sky where the crows are flying in a spiral pattern, swirling and turning like the black heart of a cyclone brewing its destructive forces. I suppress a shudder; the birds know this confrontation will be over soon – one way or the other.

Charity takes the first step towards Grace and the nun. We go with her, the heat of the amulet flowing through us. I look at the girls beside me, their faces shining, radiant, and I feel the power of life pushing through my skin.

'So you old crone, what're you going do now?' Faith asks, and I smile at the cockiness in her voice.

'She doesn't have to do anything,' Grace says, stepping to Merce's side.

My heart clenches. 'No Grace,' I say, as the power of the amulet retreats. 'Don't do this.'

'Grace?' Charity's voice falters, slipping away like water.

'Why are you surprised, Charity? We couldn't prevail against her the first time, and she killed us for our impertinence. I'm not going through that again. Not in this reality or any other. Why fight what you can't defeat?'

'But you said—'

'I was wrong.'

'But I believe in you.'

'Don't be foolish, Charity. This isn't a betrayal but an opportunity. You have lived this once, died once because of it.'

'But Hope said— '

'What do Hope and Faith know of these things?' Grace demands. 'Where were they when we needed them? We must listen to Sister. She's been here longer than us and she will be here long after unless we join her and make a new Sisterhood.' She holds out her hand to Charity. 'If you believe in me, trust the love I have for you. It is the only way.'

I feel the urge in Charity to go to her, feel her grip relax, and I don't try to stop her, though I know it'll be the end of us if she makes the choice.

Yield.

Faith doesn't share my acceptance. 'Oh what sort of lame-arsed bullshit is that?' she says. A wave of searing heat rushes through me as she turns on Charity. 'And don't you dare fall for that crap. You know it's not Grace. It's that— that thing, using her as a mouthpiece. It's afraid we're going to beat it—'

'You shouldn't speak of what you don't understand,' Grace says, cutting Faith off as she steps away from Merce, moving behind the nun so she's partly blocked from view.

'She's right child, there's no other way out of this for you,' Merce says, her eyes bright as they slide over Faith and me. This close to her, I can see the shadow of her real self; the creature of my nightmares born from the agonies of the women and girls she had consumed during her long, evil existence.

I look past the nun to Grace. I know her sudden alliance with the Sister is Merce infiltrating her mind but I still want to shake her until she wakes up from the illusion. And I would, except all I can see of her is an outstretched hand reaching for Charity.

'These other two have led you astray,' Merce continues, 'but it's not too late to return to the righteous path. God is always willing to accept you back into His house. You only need to reach out and take Grace's hand and the glory of God will once again be yours.'

'For Christ's sake, you're not buying that rubbish, are you, Charity?' Faith asks.

'She is right,' Charity says, her eyes locked onto Grace.

Overcome.

Charity takes Grace's hand.

But she doesn't let go of mine.

Surrender.

'Grace?' Faith says, a note of desperation in her voice as she reaches out for the penitent.

Their hands touch.

The circle is joined.

The power of the amulet blasts through me, separating my spirit from my body. I want to scream at the pain, but my jaw is clenched so tight I taste the grit of my teeth. The energy lifts me towards the sky amongst the crows. I can smell the musty oil of their feathers as they flap against my face and body, slicing at my skin like razor blades.

I'm bleeding, I think, but the wetness is only the rush of tears cascading over my cheeks. I try to turn my head to see the girls; are they below me? With me? Above me?

The swirling feathered mass blinds me, and I can't hear anything over the cawing, but I feel Charity and Faith's fingers pressing into mine as we rise above the crows. The velvet night greets us and there's a moment to stare in awe at the silver-blue moon, before we plummet through the blackness, drawing the light with us, into our bodies.

To be back in my body is a relief, but there's no time to enjoy it. My attention is caught by Grace. Silver-blue light pours from her eyes and mouth in delicate streams that race towards Charity and Faith, where they entwine and flow over to me.

'Devious hellcats. What have you done now?' Merce scuttles between us, looking for a way to escape but we have her corralled. She holds a hand over her eyes, shielding them from the light as she's forced into the centre of our circle. Malice twists her features. 'You think you can defeat me?' she snarls. 'You don't know who you're dealing with, but you'll learn. Oh yes, all of you *will* learn.' Raising her arms, the nun splays her fingers and stabs them towards heaven, as a chant – an old Latin prayer – pours over her lips.

I strain to follow the words, but the power rising in her distracts me.

'Sweet Jesus,' Faith murmurs.

'Steady,' I say, trying to sound reassuring.

Merce leaps towards Charity, taking her by the throat. The nun's hand and arm blister where the light touches it. A hiss fills the air as the flesh bubbles, but Merce doesn't release her grip.

Charity's eyes bulge and her mouth falls open. I want to leap on the nun and pound her head into a bloody mass but Grace – *damn her* – speaks in my mind: *Do not break the circle, lest you would condemn Charity to the black lake for all eternity.* I glare at Grace but she doesn't see; her eyes are turned to the heavens. I follow her gaze as Charity coughs and gurgles.

The crows have consolidated into a dense black cloud. I scream at them, calling on them to end our lives before Merce can extract her final revenge. And the birds come; a black stream pouring like oil out of the sky, a torrent of feathers, sharp beaks and glittering eyes. They caw in unison, a riot of screeching and squawking as they slam into the centre of us: pecking, clawing, ripping— tearing Merce apart.

Not all of them survive. They dive into the ground until the inside of our circle is littered with jittering bodies, and Merce doesn't go down without a fight. She roars from beneath the weight of the crows and grabs at the birds, squeezing them until they burst in an explosion of blood and feathers. My stomach heaves at the scent of their death, acidic and coppery, and I spit out the bitter saliva that floods my mouth.

The hand holding Charity releases its grip and swats at the birds. They respond by snapping off the nun's fingers. A digit falls to the ground and the crows leap on it, squabbling like seagulls until one grabs the prize and streaks away with a triumphant cry. Others follow, chasing the victor across the sky.

Charity staggers, sagging as she leans forward, gasping, but Faith and Grace hold her steady, refusing to allow her to break the circle until the crows have finished their grisly work.

I watch in horror as they reduce Merce to no more than a few scraps of black habit and strands of hair. It's the worst thing I've ever seen and yet I can't look away; I have to witness her destruction for all of the fallen girls who have suffered at her hands.

As the last crows flaps away, I feel the heat from the amulet fade. The light fades with it and I release Grace and Faith's hands even though it hurts; my fingers have held theirs so tightly, we seem melded into one.

Grace smiles as our circle breaks apart. 'It's done,' she says.

'She's really gone?' Charity asks, her voice a harsh

207

whisper.

Grace nods. 'Gone forever.'

The girls embrace, their smiles shining through their tears. I look over at Faith, who smiles as she wraps her arms around Grace and Charity. A moment later, I join them – my sisterhood.

We stand in each other's arms for a few minutes, enjoying the peace that comes with victory, until Grace pulls away. I look at her. My happiness fades as I realise she's become less substantial. Beside her, Charity shimmers with translucence.

'It is time for us to leave this place,' she says.

'No. Wait. Don't go yet. We need to—' Grace brushes my cheek with fingers I can't feel. 'But we should talk. What if the Sisterhood—'

Grace touches her temple. 'I will always be with you.'

'Thank you,' Charity says as Faith wraps an arm around my waist. I slip my arm over hers and watch as Grace and Charity become mist, shadow, nothing.

Sadness, deep as a cold, dark lake, fills me until I hear Grace whisper in my mind: *Always with you.*

'What do we do now?' Faith asks.

I smile – *always with the questions* – but don't answer. In the distance is a glimmer of light as the new day dawns across the back of the mountains. I feel exhilarated by the sight, but I'm also bone-weary and a yawn stretches my mouth.

'That's not very ladylike,' Faith laughs.

I grab her hand and lead her towards the church. 'C'mon, I think it's time we prayed a little.'

'What are we praying for?' Faith asks, pushing open the door.

'To get the hell outta here.'

Chapter Seven

Sister Am walks with us to the front gate. We pass the place where the Poinciana tree stood, its demise marked by a mound of freshly turned dirt where the tree-stumper's been at work. A twinge of sadness spikes my heart as the image of two other mounds of earth rises in my mind: the graves of Mary and Father Joachim.

The day they buried Father Joachim I cried heaps but, somehow, it was worse with Mary. As the clods of dirt fell on her white casket, I tasted bitter regret. Mary had been a bitch, but how much of that was her fault? The Sisters had made her what she was and we hadn't helped. All of the girls at St Mary's had participated in the Sister's evil by refusing to protect each other. Instead, we submitted to their control and surveillance. It was a surrender that had cost Mary – and countless other unfortunate girls – their lives.

I shake these thoughts from my head and look down the driveway to the car waiting at the gate. The door opens and Mama steps out. I sigh. *How much different will life be in the real world?*

'That sounds like a heavy load, Hope.'

Sister Am's voice is warm as a spring breeze. I smile at her. 'It's Amy, Sister,' I remind her.

'Of course it is,' she says, and pats my arm. 'Sorry, my dear,' she says as two more cars pulled up at the gate: a Mercedes behind my mother's car and the other, a shiny BMW in military green, on the opposite side of the street.

Heather groans. 'Why did she have to bring *him*?' she says as a man in a plaid sports coat and white tennis shoes dashes around the car and opens the door. A woman in a figure-hugging dress steps onto the street. Heather groans again. 'Brilliant.'

'For two girls who are about to go home, there appears to be a great deal of pessimism,' Sister Am admonishes gently.

'You're right, Sister. Maybe we should stay,' Heather says and starts to turn back to the dormitory.

Sister Am laughs and takes her by the arm. 'Oh no, my dear, there is no place here for you now. You've done enough.'

I glance at the nun; it's the first time she's even hinted at the events of the last week. She smiles benevolently and I remember the worry in her eyes when I woke in the church to find her leaning over me.

I moaned as I sat up, feeling like I'd been pounded with a baseball bat. Heather was slumped in the pew beside me; her skin alabaster, chest motionless. I touched her arm. It was cold beneath my fingers. I felt a flutter of fear in my stomach and, ignoring the protest from my throbbing hands, I grabbed her shoulders and shook her.

'Oi, get outtov it,' she muttered as her eyes flicked open. She pushed me away with a hiss and cupped her hands to her chest.

'Oh thank God you're alright,' Sister Am said. 'I thought you were— No, never mind. You're okay and that's all that matters.' She gathered us into her arms and helped us through the church.

The sun was brilliant and I had to squint until my

eyes adjusted as we shuffled down the steps and through the church grounds. I tried to find evidence of the destruction we had brought to the Sisterhood but everything looked as it usually did. There were no scorch marks, no broken gates, no more crows than usual. I snuck a glance at Heather and saw the dismay on her face.

Was it real?

Then we came to the Poinciana.

A sob broke from Heather and Sister Am let go of me to embrace her. Heather cried into the nun's shoulder as I stared at the old tree. It had succumbed completely, pulling its roots from the earth as it fell, crushing branches and scattering leaves across the grass. I stepped closer, feeling the need to touch the burn marks that scarred its bark.

Real.

'Something has left here,' Sister Am said, placing her hand on my shoulder. 'The work is done and it's time for you to rest.' She walked us to the dormitory and saw us into our beds, where we slept undisturbed until the morning of Mary and Father Joachim's funerals.

After the ceremony, Heather came over and took my hand, gripping it like a lost child. I held her just as tight.

'Are you okay?' she asked.

'Guess so. I was thinking of Caleb.'

'Oh,' Heather said, and inched closer until our shoulders were touching, giving me the comfort of her presence...

'Are you ready to go girls?' Sister Am says. The nun's voice brings me back to the present. I push the events of the last week away, sending my thoughts of Caleb with them.

At the bottom of the driveway, Mama waits. She raises a welcoming hand. *That's unexpected*, I think, waving in return. *Where has this friendliness come from?* Then I see a movement inside the car and understand; another boyfriend. I lower my hand and slow my steps, as reluctant as Heather to leave St Mary's.

The doors to the car behind Mama's opens and a couple dressed in expensive coats step into the street, followed by a blonde girl of about fifteen. She stands apart from them, body stiff, hair falling over her face. Her mother reaches out and brushes it away with an irritated swipe.

Sister Am clicks her tongue and coos like a mother seeing her newborn child for the first time. 'That must be Sophia. What a joy it is to have her join us,' she says, quickening her step. 'Come girls.'

Heather and I follow reluctantly. 'Is that Jeremy?' I ask, nodding to the geek standing beside the BMW.

'Yep. And it looks like your mum has a new friend too,' she says, nodding towards the car.

'Seems so. Nothing really changes, does it?'

Heather stops. 'We changed something.'

I look into her eyes, see the reassurance she needs and smile. 'Damn straight. We kicked arse.'

A movement from the limousine catches my eye. The door opens and a person appears beside the car.

'Oh my God!' Heather says, as I take off running, not hearing the admonishment from Sister Am as I scramble past her.

My mouth presses against his before I can say his name.

'Okay that's enough,' Sister Am says, as she and my mother pull us apart.

'Yes, let's have a little decorum,' Mama agrees.

I ignore them and reach for his face, touching his skin, marvelling at its warmth. 'Caleb? How can this be? You came to me in my dream and I thought you had died, but you're here. How can it be?'

Caleb gives me an uncertain smile. 'Well, the doctor said it was touch and go, but it'd take more than some dirty ice to take me out. I'm tougher than that, you know,' he says, the smile turning cheeky as he looks over at Mama.

My glance moves between them and I feel a wave of confusion at their apparent camaraderie. 'What? So you guys are best buddies now. How the hell did that happen?'

'Watch your language, Amy,' Sister Am says.

Caleb touches my shoulder and the warmth of his hand makes me shiver. 'After that day at your house, I hit the rollercoaster hard for a week and eventually, got knocked on my arse. Your mum found me—'

'I had a few more things to say to him,' Mama says.

Caleb smiles at her. 'Lucky for me, 'cause she got me to the hospital. I was in a coma for a bit, but your mum,' he moves his hand to touch my cheek, 'she saved my life.'

I turn to Mama, stunned. Then Father Joachim speaks in my mind, delivering his simple truth: *Love is the one thing that unites us all, Amy. Believe and accept.* My heart swells. Mama holds out her arms to me but I don't get the chance to go to her as Heather's mother strides between us in a waft of *Poison*.

'Family reunions are overrated,' she says, grabbing Heather by the arm and dragging her towards the waiting BMW. 'Let's go young lady. I have a plane to catch.'

I take hold of Heather's hand as she shuffles by, pulling her to a stop. Her mother turns towards me and I wait for her to give me a mouthful. I can see she wants to, but Caleb and Mama are standing behind me.

'One minute, Heather, and not a second longer,' she snaps, stalking over to the car.

'Bitch,' Heather says.

'Yeah,' I agree, and hug her. 'Look, if it gets too much, you've got a place with me.' I look at Mama for confirmation and she nods.

'Thanks Amy, for everything,' Heather says, as the BMW starts up.

I kiss her cheek and hug her again. Then she's running across the road and slipping into the car. She pushes her hand against the back window in a last goodbye as the BMW follows the Mercedes around the corner.

'What a gift to have such a good friend,' Sister Am says and I turn to her, smiling.

Beside Sister Am, the new girl is looking at the ground, trying to hide the tears shimmering on her eyelashes. I want to tell her everything will be okay, that things are good now, that Sister Am will look after her, but Mama and Caleb are waiting.

'Ready to go?' Mama asks.

'Oh, it's definitely time for her to go,' Sister Am says.

Tiny fingers of unease creep up my back as I look into the Sister's eyes and see something dark and familiar shifting in their depths. 'No,' I whisper.

'It's okay Dao-girl, you're free now,' Caleb says, leading me to the car.

As I climb in, I hear a familiar recital: *We are governed by rules here. You will learn the rules and learn them quickly. Failure to abide by the rules will result in a punishment...* As Sister Am speaks, she looks at me, a sly grin on her face.

I buzz down the window. 'Don't give up hope, Sophia,' I call.

'Your time is done,' Sister Am responds as the car pulls away. High above her, a crow screams and I know, deep inside where my voices speak to me, that the nun and Caleb are wrong.

I'm not finished with the Sisterhood.

Not yet.

Acknowledgments

Excerpt from The Handmaid's Tale by Margaret Atwood. Copyright © 1986 by O.W. Toad Ltd. Reprinted by permission of Houghton Mifflin Harcourt Publishing Company. All rights reserved; Reprinted by permission of McClelland & Stewart, a division of Random House of Canada Limited, a Penguin Random House Company; Published by Vintage. Reprinted by permission of The Random House Group Ltd.

Excerpt from speech by Leymah Roberta Gbowee, Nobel Peace Laureate 2011 © The Nobel Foundation.

MIRA FALLING

MARIA ARENA

Mira Falling dreams of becoming a star... but achieving fame and fortune can be difficult when you're stuck in a dead-end town like Harvest Bay and have a brilliant brother who overshadows your every move.

When Sebastian Holborn and his wealthy family move into the house across the street, Mira sees an opportunity for escape and for the fame she desires, but Sebastian's scheming twin sister, Lily, has other ideas.

Mira, however, knows there is a solution to every problem, and she will allow nothing and no one to stand in the way of her dream.

To purchase *Mira Falling* or read more about Maria Arena, visit: www.mariaarena.com.au